Arianna Snow's The Lochmoor Glen Series

"Patience, My Dear is an enthralling, well crafted, superbly written 'page-turner' of a read, fruitfully exposed to the impairing remembrance and encounter of a first young love when nearing mid-life many years later. *Patience, My Dear* is very strongly recommended for readers searching for a superbly authored telling of an intricate and entertaining tale involving a love consumed memory and an ever-deepening mystery."

"A comedy of errors held together with taut suspense and biting dialogue, *My Magic Square* is a delicious pleasure from beginning to end."

"Unwelcome visitors make their residence nearby, and there's a reason why they're unwelcome. *Threaded Needles* follows two amateur detectives whose bond of blood is unbreakable as they try to find out just what suspicious character Ian MacGill and his associate are planning. The resulting adventure is entertaining and enthralling. *Threaded Needles* is highly recommended for community library mystery collections."

"A compelling human drama unfolds, making *Blessed Petals* a very solidly recommended read."

"Without a Sword   is another entry into the Lochmoor Glen series, and does the series justice."

"Another exciting thriller from Arianna Snow, *Kade* is not a read to be missed for fans of the series."

"A gripping read of drama, *Please, Tell Me* is a top pick and very highly recommended."

"Geoffrey's Secret is a must for lovers of historical fiction and the flavor of the 1800s."

"For those who have enjoyed the previous entries into the series or dramas surrounding socialites, *Each Rising Tide* is a fine pick, not to be overlooked." **—Midwest Book Review**

Life Without You

A NOVEL

Arianna Snow

Golden Horse Ltd.
Davis City, Iowa

This book is primarily a book of fiction. Names, characters, places and incidents are either products of the author's imagination or actual historic places and events, which have been used fictitiously for historical reference, as noted.

An Original Publication of Golden Horse Ltd.
Davis City, IA 50065 U.S.A.

www.ariannaghnovels.com
ISBN 13: 9781513604398

Library of Congress Control Number: 2015952327
First Printing
Volume 14 of *The Lochmoor Glen Series*

Printed and bound in the United States of America
by Publishers' Graphics, LLC, Carol Stream, IL

Cover: Photography by DLO
        Printed by White Oak Printing, Lancaster PA

♥

In Memory
of
Aunt Bernie Fasnacht

With
Love and Admiration
for a woman who blessed this world
with her incredible Strength,
an inspiring positive Attitude,
and a delightful sense of Humor.
All who knew her, loved her.
We all should be so fortunate
to leave behind such a legacy.

My Special thanks to :
GOD

KAEZ
(editorial work for the *entire* series—
I could not have done it without you!)

David O., family and friends
(support)

Momma and Daddy
(packaging)

David Miller for supervision
of cover production for series

HIRAM GEOFFREY MCDONNALLY FAMILY TREE

PATERNAL GRANDPARENTS
CAPTAIN GEOFFREY EDWARD MCDONNALLY

CATHERINE NORTON MCDONNALLY

FATHER
CAPTAIN GEOFFREY LACHLAN MCDONNALLY

UNCLE
EDWARD CALEB MCDONNALLY

MATERNAL GRANDPARENTS
ALEXANDER THOMAS SELRACH

SARAH GLASGOW SELRACH

MOTHER
AMANDA SELRACH MCDONNALLY

SISTER
HANNAH RUTH MCDONNALLY

> FIANCEE: OSCAR CANDOLE

NIECE
SOPHIA RUTH SIERZIK

> HUSBAND: RAHZVON M. SIERZIK

> CHILDREN: ZANYA, VONMANSTRONG, RUTHIA

CARETAKERS
ALBERT ZIGMANN ELOISE ZIGMANN

SON - GUILLAUME ZIGMANN

> FRIENDS: TRINA DUNMORE, MERCEDES M.STOCKDALE

LIVIA NICHOLS (much better half)

COLLEAGUE: JOEL MERRIMAN

NAOMI BEATRICE (MACKENZIE) MCDONNALLY FAMILY TREE

PATERNAL GRANDPARENTS

JEREMIAH NORMAN MACKENZIE

OCTAVIA HILL MACKENZIE

FATHER

NATHAN ELIAS MACKENZIE

DAGMAR ARNOLDSON MACKENZIE (STEPMOTHER)

MATERNAL GRANDPARENTS

JAMES HENRY SMITHFIELD

IRENE CLEBOURNE SMITHFIELD

MOTHER

BEATRICE SMITHFIELD MACKENZIE (Birdie)

 DANIEL O'LEARDON

BROTHER

JEREMIAH JAMES MACKENZIE

DAUGHTER

ALLISON SARAH O'CONNOR

HUSBAND

EDWARD CALEB MCDONNALLY

HALF-BROTHER

HENRY STRICKLAND (SON OF CECIL AND BEATRICE)

 WIFE: PEARL SONS: MARVIN, CONRAD

FRIENDS

HARRIET DUGAN, JOSEPH DUGAN, HENRY J. MCTAVISH (Tavy)/

   RUFUS

MARYANNE AND BRUCE WHEATON

DAUGHTERS: WILMOTH, MARVEL, CORINNE, JEANIE, DARA, MARTHA

The Chapters

Chapter I

"Gone Fishing"

"I stretch my arms to the
unanswering heavens,
'Tis empty space,—no form,
No shape is here!
I call,—no answer to my cry is given,
Powerless my voice falls on
Night's laden ear!"

—Pamela S. Vining

Hiram McDonnally carried the reclaimed orphan, Thomas "Kade" Brenin through the garden adorning the south façade of McDonnally Manor. The master could not be more surprised at the outcome of Lieutenant Brenin's visit. He had relinquished all rights to the toddler, as the soldier had been disabled while serving in the war and his wife had taken ill. Hiram, who had made a previous attempt to adopt the child as an infant, after the mother's demise in a cart accident in Hiram's drive, was the primary candidate for the position of Kade's caretaker.

Hiram approached his fiancé, Livia Nichols, without a second thought for the other homeless orphan, Rufus, who shared the gazebo swing with her. The two had been waiting for Hiram's return and approval of Rufus's adoption. Rufus, too, had tragically lost his parents only a short time before.

However, upon seeing Hiram with Kade, Livia left Rufus and rushed to them. The couple shared the next several minutes doting over the new addition to their soon to be family. Kade, initially reserved on acquaintance with his new mother, clung to Hiram's jacket lapel. However, Livia's sweet, comforting words quickly won him over.

While the minutes passed, young, distraught Rufus had left the gazebo and moved farther away from the estate. Darting haphazardly through a screen of tears, he headed east through the woods dividing the McDonnally estates. He paused at the forest's edge, glancing back in hopes of seeing Livia in desperate pursuit; such was not the case. In fact, she had disappeared with Hiram and Kade. Rufus continued fearlessly into the shadows of the oaks looming above. He now had little regard for his safety; in his opinion, his life had already come to an end. His pace became slower in the enveloping darkness; he slid his leather soles before him, feeling for any obstructions. Streams of starlight prevented several mishaps with fallen logs. The black canopy intensified his sense of diminutiveness and insignificance; he was really nothing now; no one cared whether he lived or died. He was alone—no parents, no family, no loved ones, no friends. He stepped into the clearing in front of Brachney Hall, the home of Hiram's Uncle Edward and wife Naomi, which appeared to be lifeless; no lights were burning.

He noted a figure standing on the opposite bank of the pond at the south end of the mansion. Suddenly Rufus was spotted; the man was waving at him. He quickly ducked into the shadows. The man had dropped his fishing pole and was running around the pond towards him. Rufus panicked, running deeper into the woods. Where was the path? Branches grabbed his shirt, while his spindly arms did little to block his face as he pushed forward, stumbling over rocks and unfamiliar deterrents. It was hopeless. He fell to the ground. Frantically, he pulled at the entwining stems that snaked about his ankles. He worked madly until he was free; his heart was pounding in his ears and his sobs were muffling any sounds about him. He had just stood up to run when there *he* was, the man from before. There was no escaping the enormous stalker. In his attempt to run, a tight grip on his shirt deterred him.

"Laddie, ye need not be afraid. What are ye doin' in the timber at this time o' night?" the man gently asked.

After a brief struggle, the man lifted him and carried him to the clearing, then lowered him to the ground with a precautionary grip on Rufus's forearm. Rufus was now, face-to-face with the squatting captor.

"Who are ye, laddie?"

"Nobody," Rufus mumbled.

"Does yer ma and pa know ye'r out here?"

"I have no Ma and Pa."

"Where's yer kin?"

"I have no kin. I dunna have nobody—let go o' me arm!"

"Only if ye dunna move."

Rufus nodded. The man released him. Rufus shot away. Quick as he was, he was no match for the long-legged pursuer. Once again, he was swept off his feet.

"Laddie, ye'r comin' wi' me. The McDonnallys will take ye in for the night."

He hauled the defiant, flailing wiggle worm up to Brachney Hall and dropped him on the back step.

"What fix are ye in, son? What hae ye done?"

"Nothin', I tell ye!"

"Keep yer voice down." The man grasped him by the shoulders. "Then ye hae no reason to run. What is yer name? I believe that I hae seen ye before."

"What's yers?" Rufus asked indignantly.

"Tavy—Henry McTavish."

"I hae n' name. I am nobody."

"Aye. Where is yer family?"

"Heaven—not that it be any business o' yers."

"I am sorry to hear that. Maybe they are visitin' me ma and pa."

Rufus cocked his head with curiosity.

"Aye, me parents hae been gone for some time."

"Were they old?"

"Nay, I was young when I lost 'em. I am an orphan, but I hae the Dugans."

"That ol' busy body Harriet?"

"*Eh*? I love the woman like she was me natural Ma. She is a good woman and I willna stand for anyone bad mouthin' her."

Rufus's eyes widened fearfully. "Sorry, sir."

"Apology accepted. Call me Tavy."

"How did ye get 'em to take ye in?"

"A few years ago when I came to Lochmoor Glen, not knowin' anyone, they just took me under their wings."

"Oh." Rufus looked at the ground for a moment. Then he glanced off in the general direction of the pond. "Did ye catch anythin'?"

Tavy smiled. "Nay, just drownin' worms."

"Why were ye fishin' in the night?"

"Sometimes it quiets me soul. I hae a lot on me mind."

"Me, too."

"What's troublin' ye?"

"I thought I found me family...like ye and the Dukans—but that brat came back and they choosed him."

"Brat?"

"That brat, Kade."

"Kade? The McDonnally Kade?"

"'Tis the one."

"Kade's back. Hmm?"

"I loved Miss Nichols and I thought she loved me—but n' more," he said downcast.

"People hae room for many loves in their heart."

"Not after what she did to me—once they break yer heart—ye canna love 'em n' more."

Tavy stared curiously at the young philosopher. "Aye—I understand how ye feel. 'Tis late and ye need a place to bunk. What is yer objection to Naomi and Edward?"

"Obnection?"

"Do ye mind stayin' wi' 'em?"

"Aye. They're Donnallys."

"Aye they are. Ye can come home wi' me."

"I dunna think I can. Mrs. Dukan doesna take to me."

"Why is that?"

"Her cake at the church..." Rufus trailed off, remembering the embarrassing event.

Tavy laughed. "Ma Dugan has a bit o' a temper, but she's a forgivin' woman. Come along, I'll protect ye from her wrath."

"What's that?" Rufus backed away.

"Dunna worry." He took Rufus's little hand in his. "Me horse is o'er there."

"Dunna say I didna warn ye."

Tavy smiled and pulled Rufus up behind him. They rode slowly off to the Dugan cottage.

Not quite sure how Ma Dugan would react to the little "afters" destroyer, Tavy left Rufus on the back step while he attempted to soft-soap her.

"Evenin', Ma."

"Did ye catch a big one?"

"Nay...a wee one."

"Where is it?" she said, scanning his person.

"On the back porch."

"Well, bring it in."

Tavy nodded and reluctantly went to fetch the day's catch. He opened the door and Rufus stepped over the kitchen threshold.

"Agh! Get that scamp out o' me kitchen!"

Tavy grabbed a hold of Rufus before he fled for cover.

"Ma, he has no place to go; both o' his parents hae passed. He is all alone in the world," Tavy pleaded.

"And he can be alone elsewhere! Out o' here!"

Tavy led Rufus outside and explained, "She needs time to get use to the idea."

"She is old. She doesna hae that much time."

Tavy chuckled. "I hae been feelin' a bit cooped up in the house. What ye say to bunkin' in the barn?" He cupped his ear to Ma Dugan's muffled rantings. "Besides it will be quieter out here."

Rufus returned a grin.

"Wait here. I'll get some blankets."

Tavy started to pull his hand from Rufus's, but Rufus held tight.

"Trust me. I will be back in a blink o' an eye."

"Better, or mine will be closed."

Once the two were bedded down next to the mule, Jock, in the adjoining stall, Tavy spoke quietly, "Carrot Top, we need to pay a visit to Hiram's, in the mornin'. They'll be lookin' for ye."

"Carrot tops are green."

"Aye, and ye are. Ye'r young and ye need to be listenin' to me. Do as I say—ye understand?"

"Tavy, maybe I should stay wi' ye...since ye hae to sleep in the barn, ye might be lonely."

"Goodnight, Rufus. 'Tis late."

"How did ye know me name?"

"Ma. She is quite familiar wi' it."

Tavy and Rufus arrived at the McDonnally estate shortly after eight o'clock, the following morning. Tavy reached over and handed the reins to Rufus who sat in the cart next to him. Tavy noted the little trembling fingers as Rufus spoke.

"I'll wait here for ye. I dunna want to see any o' them."

"Aye."

Tavy jumped from the cart and seconds later he disappeared through the front door. Rufus wrapped and unwrapped the reins around his hand. After a few minutes, he climbed down and sought refuge on the front step. He sat up when he saw a little figure of female persuasion skipping down the drive toward him. It was a Wheaton girl, but not his beloved Jeanie.

"Hello, Rufus."

"Mornin', Corinne."

"What are ye doin' here?"

"Waitin."

"Waitin' for what?"

"Tavy."

"Oh. I am here to deliver a note to Mrs. McDonnally."

Rufus jumped up. His worst nightmare had come true. "*Mrs.* Donnally?" he stuttered.

"I mean Miss Nichols."

Rufus sat back down with a sigh of relief.

"Wilmoth, may have to miss some school and help Ma wi' puttin' up the vegetables this year." She hopped up two steps. "'Tis grand 'bout Naomi McDonnally, is it not?"

"What 'bout her?"

"She's havin' a bairn," she grinned.

"Anot'er *family*," he said, dropping his head into his hands, resting on his knees.

"What is wrong wi' a family? I think 'tis excitin' news."

"I dunna think so."

Corinne shrugged and bounded up the last step. She was stretching to reach the doorknocker when Tavy stepped out. Rufus turned and slowly rose at seeing Tavy's concerned countenance.

"What happened?" Rufus asked in a barely audible voice.

"Nothin' ye need to worry 'bout. We need to get back for chores."

Tavy lifted Rufus into the cart and climbed up.

"'Tis a complicated situation," Tavy added, holding the reins, staring across the moors.

The atmosphere in the McDonnally mansion was thick with tension. The walls of Hiram's study ached with the ongoing conflict.

"Hiram, you are being positively unreasonable," Livia charged.

"Unreasonable? I am not going to have Kade, an innocent child who has suffered more than his share in his short life, exposed to the danger and ill behavior of that little beggar!"

"*Rufus* is an innocent child, too—a victim of circumstances—an orphan who needs a home, as much as Kade does. He only misbehaves to gain love and attention."

"He can misbehave elsewhere. You heard McTavish. He is looking after the lad."

"He kept him for one night. That is all. You cannot expect Henry, a single man, to take responsibility for a little boy."

"Well, I *am* single, as yet," Hiram countered.

"Is that a threat?"

"Nay, Livy." He walked over and gently grasped her shoulders. "I understand your concern for the lad and I do hope he finds a decent home, but Kade is young. We have the wedding and settling him in. You are busy with the school. Is that not enough?"

"And what about Rufus? Daniel said that there is no one to take him."

"I promised LT. Brenin to take Kade and raise him properly. I am certain that someone will take the lad in."

"There is no one, Hiram." She turned and left the study.

"Where are you going?"

"To get Rufus."

Livia ran to the portal and called to the slow moving cart, ambling down the drive with Jock in the lead. After a few words with Tavy, she was helping Rufus down from the cart. Livia took Rufus's hand in hers and entered the McDonnally mansion.

To appease Hiram, Livia immediately began the search for a home for Rufus. It was not long before she realized that it was futile; his reputation preceded him. His convictions for terrorizing the community were common knowledge and few offered any sympathy for his attempts to "gain love and attention."

From Rufus's perspective, there were only two

caring people in his world—Livia and Joel, the attentive schoolmaster who took a special interest in Rufus, the boy who idolized his dear friend Livia. Rufus lived in Hiram's home and spent his waking moments under the care and instruction of the two schoolteachers. Tavy had returned to the Dugan family and Rufus had forgiven Livia, with hopes of a second chance at becoming her son. As Joel was unattached and adored Livia, Rufus thought that the three of them made the perfect *family.* Rufus planned to take advantage of Kade's return. Kade would be the perfect distraction for Hiram while Rufus regained a place in his surrogate mother's heart.

Late one afternoon, Hiram cleaned up after his rounds at the farms and then checked on the slumbering Kade. With Gantwell, his faithful canine companion, trotting at his side, Hiram ventured to the academically refurbished west wing to see Livia. He opened the door and peeked inside. A couple of voices and quiet laughter drew his attention to the far wall overlooking the play yard. Joel and Rufus were helping Livia to her feet. Livia was retrieving an oversized picture book from the floor.

"Now, young man," Livia addressed Rufus, "you be a perfect gentleman at supper with Mr. Merriman."

Rufus smiled up at her. "I will, Mummy." He kissed her hand.

Mummy? Hiram's muscles tensed.

"Rufus, my name is Miss Nichols. Now, I shall see you later tonight. Make him mind, Joel." Livia grinned.

Rufus pulled on Joel's hand. "Come along, Daddy. You said we could go to the toyshop first."

Joel shook his head and smiled. "Yes, son, come a—" Joel looked up to see Hiram's unwelcoming expression. "Hello, Mr. McDonnally. She is all yours. We are off to supper." He pulled Rufus through the door.

Rufus was contesting, "She is not—she is ours! Our Mummy!"

"Shh!" Joel warned and closed the door behind them.

Hiram, silently watched Livia return the book to the shelf.

She looked up. "Well then, all I have to do is throw a few things in the dustbin and I will be done for the day." She glanced nervously at Hiram. "Is Kade still napping?"

"Aye...That is the last time I will be witness to that, *Mummy*."

She closed the light in the school kitchen and approached him. "What are you implying?" she asked innocently.

"I am not *implying* anything. Simply, your days as Rufus's *mummy* are over. Kade is your only son."

"Do not be absurd," she said casually and led the way to the hall. "Rufus is just reaching out to a mother figure."

"The lad is confused. Extending his stay will do more harm than good, in the long run...for all of us. You need to make other arrangements, Livy."

"You know that is impossible. There is no one."

"I beg to differ with you. He has obviously

adopted you and your colleague to be his parents!"

"Naturally, he is searching to fill that void."

"Mr. Merriman is going to have to raise him, alone. There is plenty of room at the inn."

"A little boy growing up at the inn?" she objected.

"Growing up? Aye, you expected him to live out his appalling youth to manhood under my roof! I shan't have it, Livy. He detests me and is set on disrupting every moment that I have available with you and Kade—which I might remind you are few and far between!"

"At least give us time to find a proper home for him."

"Us? I shall not waste another minute on the subject."

"I was referring to Joel and myself."

"So *us* is the two of you?"

"That is not what I meant." She wrung her hands. "You are twisting my words."

"Livy, the only twisting being done is by that young scallywag who is determined to break off our engagement and make a home with you and '*Daddy'!* I am finished for the day, as well. Good day, *Miss* Nichols."

Gantwell barked at her twice and pranced off behind her master. Livia held back her tears and reached for her handkerchief in the pocket of her cardigan. Her hand fell on a piece of paper. She pulled it out and opened it. Her brows knitted. It was a sketch of two stick figures, one bearing some resemblance to a man and the other to a woman donning a triangular skirt. Both were wearing extraordinarily large smiles. The elongated digits of the hands met those of the small figure between them. Her gaze fell to the far left bottom corner of the paper. The artist's mark—a tiny disproportioned, uppercase "R."

"Oh *Rufus*, what am I to do?"

Chapter II

"To a Tea"

"A sense of humour, and a touch of mirth,
To brighten up the shadowy spots of earth;
And pride that passes evil—choosing good.
All these unite in perfect womanhood."

—Ella Wheeler Wilcox

That evening, at the Sierzik home, Rahzvon was sprawled across the couch with daughter Zanya asleep on his chest. His wife, Sophia sat on a blanket spread on the floor. She was divvying out wooden blocks to the other two of the triplets, Ruthia and her brother Von.

She spoke in her usual enthusiasm, "Just think little ones, you will soon have not one, but two little friends to play with: Kade and Uncle Edward's baby. It will be awhile before he or she can romp around with you—oh, romp means run around—roll around—no matter." She clapped her hands together. "In no time you will all be the best of friends."

She glanced to the mantle, to the mystery picture of the couple and a young boy. She had found it in her yard after the twister. Distracted by its presence, she thought, *Someone will surely recognize you.* She then looked over to her sleeping husband and touched his arm.

"Rahzie? Rahzie, wake up."

"Uh?" he stirred, his eyes still closed. "I am sorry. I did not mean to muss your red ringlet," he mumbled.

The black haired Sophia froze. Her eyes widened; her jaw dropped.

All was silent for nearly two full seconds before the mischievous husband's eyes flashed open, "Only teasing," he grinned.

"I am sick to death of that woman with the red ringlets! If you were not wearing the protective armor of our daughter, you would be grinning at the floor!"

He scooted up to a sitting position, taking care not to waken Zanya.

"Sorry, Phia. I could not resist," he snickered. "You know that woman was Edward's fabrication."

"No matter. I do *not* appreciate your appalling sense of humor. Come along, it is late. Let us get these three tucked in."

Several minutes later, they kissed their babies good night and stood over the sleeping cherubs.

"I wonder how tall they will be as adults..." Sophia whispered. Rahzvon only smiled.

He followed her to their room where he plopped down on the bed with a copy of the *Navy & Army Magazine*. Sophia stood before the mirror of the mammoth wardrobe.

"Rahzie, do you think that I should bob my hair?"

He glanced up from the periodical. "Do what to your hair?"

"Bob it."

"Bob it like a draft horse's tail?"

"It is the latest fashion. What do you think?" she said, folding up her hair to chin length.

"No."

"Why not? Do you not think that I have a face for short hair? Rahzvon?"

"Yes, you have a nice face," he mumbled.

"Mr. Sierzik, you are not listening to me."

"Yes, I am."

"Would you court me, now?" she said, dropping her hair to her shoulders.

"Court you? I think that we are a little beyond that."

"No, would you court me, if we met for the first time, today?"

"With three children? Not a chance."

She walked in front of him. "What is wrong with my three beautiful children?"

"A little more than I care to take on as a *single* man."

She turned away and muttered, "Sometimes they are too much for me."

He lowered the magazine, taken aback by her serious tone. "Miss McDonnally, would you be the mother of my children?" he said, hoping to cheer her up.

She stood before the mirror, again. "Silly man...Trina's hair is bobbed and that was quite a drastic change for a former ballerina," Sophia persisted.

"You are not a ballerina."

"I could be one," she said defensively.

He shrugged.

"What does that mean?" she asked indignantly.

"Ballerinas are generally taller, aren't they?"

"Trina is *not* that tall."

"Phia, she is at least a foot taller than you."

"Are you suggesting that because I have not had training in ballet, I cannot bob my hair?"

He looked up from the magazine, completely baffled.

"No, Phia that is *not* what I am saying." He put down the magazine and slid from the bed. He placed his hands on her shoulders, and then moved his fingers to the shiny black tresses, cascading over her shoulders.

"You, Little One, have the most beautiful hair that I have ever seen. It would be a crime to take scissors to it."

"Bobbing my hair won't change anything,

anyway… You are right, I am not a ballerina, I am a mother of three…that is all," she grumbled.

"Mrs. Sierzik, you need not be tall or a prima ballerina to dance. I have watched you. You are a delightful dancer, full of grace."

"Thank you," she mumbled.

He took her hand and led her to the bed. They sat down.

"Now, Little Mother, let me braid this gorgeous head of hair. If it were short, I would lose my treasured job as NHB."

"NHB?"

"Night Hair Braider."

He retrieved a ribbon from the night table drawer and began making one thick braid.

"Rahzie, my mother is very tall."

"Yes, she is. Being Hiram's twin, it is expected."

"That means that, quite possibly, my father was short."

"Not necessarily. However, there may have been a tendency for shorter people on his side of the family."

"I wonder what he looks like. Mother refuses to talk about him."

"I would say, for the most part, you appear to be primarily of the McDonnally clan. You share all of their traits—obstinacy, temperamental—" he teased.

His comment went unnoticed; she did not retaliate. She simply replied, "I am glad my children know their father."

"Me, too." He tied the red ribbon in a neat bow at the end of the braid. "There—another masterpiece."

She walked back to the mirror. "You *have* become an expert."

"I should be, after all these nights."

She turned to him. "Do you miss your parents?"

"Yes."

"And Gaelon?"

"I miss the brother that I thought I had."

"I miss the father for the father I had hoped he would have been." She climbed into bed.

"Do you want to read for a while?" he asked.

"You go ahead, I have to think about what meals to prepare for tomorrow."

"Alright." He slid beneath the coverlet and continued reading his magazine.

Preparing meals. That is all I am. A cook, mother and housekeeper. Everyone who sees me thinks, there's Sophia, mother of the triplets. I am more than that. I am me. I can do more than tend to my babies. She glanced over at Rahzvon. *I am still young!* She focused on the mystery picture sitting on the bureau. *Who are you? I just have to find them.*

She lay silent for a quarter hour, and then sat up with a start.

"Rahzie, I want to host a tea for Naomi, honoring her mother-to-beness," Sophia said excitedly.

He laughed, "Her what? She has been a mother to Allison for years."

"You men never understand."

"Ask again in six months, when the baby is here."

"No, before it is born—to cheer her up. It is such a long process."

"Phia, you know that you do not have to ask my permission."

"I was not; I need you to take care of the children. Dear, it would be impossible to host a tea with three children underfoot," she explained.

"Do you plan on leaving them lying around the floor?" he said, with a hint of sarcasm.

"You know what I meant." She folded her hands. "Yes, a week from Saturday! You will be home from your postal route, later that afternoon."

"Who is to take care of them until I finish my route?"

"Uncle Hiram."

"*Hiram*? Oh, he will be ecstatic at that proposition."

"No, no you shan't ask him. He might refuse. Let's see...You shall pay him an unexpected visit—with our three beautiful bairns and then finish your route."

"I suppose Eloise could assist."

"No, Dear, she may be Uncle's housekeeper, but she is nearly family. She will be at the tea."

"Are you inviting Allision and Mercy—Guillaume's 'past and present'?"

"Yes, yes I am," she said with renewed confidence.

"Will you be passing out hen goggles?"

"Hen goggles?"

"I told you about them—the protective goggles so that—"

"Never you mind!"

"I can only imagine how this shall go." He shook his head and looked to the ceiling.

She looked at him with wonder. "I love you Rahzie. It will be perfect, just like you!"

"Yes I am. I am the only man who would tolerate such silly, feminine notions." He pulled her close and kissed her with unquestionable passion that only a man in love could offer.

She pulled away and jumped from the bed.

"Wait! Where are you going?"

"To get some note paper, of course! I haven't much time to plan for this party!"

That Saturday, Sophia prepared for the well-orchestrated tea, while Rahzvon headed for the Manor, albeit dubiously.

The meticulous hostess had gone to great lengths to create special party favors for each guest. The little tulle bags holding homemade candies were tied with pink and blue satin bows attached to a tiny bouquet of dried flowers. The party favors arranged carefully in a basket, sat next to an elaborate floral centerpiece on an adjoining table. Trays of little heart-shaped sandwiches, creatively pared fruits, and a cake fringed with an excessive number of pink and blue bows to match the party favors, adorned the dining room table.

Sophia took one last look in the large wardrobe mirror before her guests were due to arrive.

"Sophia Sierzik," she addressed her reflection, "that fat face is back. Only one sandwich and one wee piece of cake." She cocked her head. "Very well, one medium sized piece, we do not want the others to think that I am self-conscience of my weight." She frowned and smoothed her black eyebrows. "Perhaps two sandwiches, since they are so very tiny."

She studied the likeness of the mother of three from head to toe. "Hmm? Tolerable." She turned sideways. Her brows furrowed. "I'll have to keep my distance from that pencil Allison." She gave a wave of disgust at her profile. "Only one sandwich." She grabbed the unclaimed framed picture and headed downstairs.

Everything looked perfect. The peaceful atmosphere was amazing. Beaming with pride at her gala creations, she rushed to the window.

"They're coming!" She clapped her hands with delight.

Within minutes, the Sierzik parlor was buzzing with feminine voices. Once the last guest arrived (her mother Hannah) Sophia spoke briefly with Mercy and welcomed her guests.

"Good afternoon, ladies, and welcome to my home for this special gathering in honor of my dear friend and aunt, Naomi." All smiled at the guest of honor. "I am sorry to report that Mercy has just informed me that her employer, Mrs. Stewart, will not be joining us...due to an arthritis episode." A sigh of disappointment ran through the crowd.

She continued, "Now being an occasion to celebrate the upcoming precious...blessed event you will take note that the décor is accented in pink and blue."

The guests scanned the room, admiring the looped pink and blue bunting.

"Now, ladies, I have a special surprise for you, today, but before I reveal it, I would like you all to take a moment to examine this photograph," she explained, holding it up for all to see.

The guests grumbled with discontent.

"Some surprise," Allison interjected. "We have all seen it and are frankly tired of hearing about it," she muttered.

Taken aback by Allison's candid insolence, Sophia nonchalantly retreated and carefully stood the frame next to the party favors.

"Please examine it one more time. It may mean a great deal to those in it, to have it returned to them...now, for the surprise!"

Her audience straightened in their seats—that is all but Allison; she merely looked to her cuff and straightened her sleeve. Sophia's eyes narrowed at Allison's act of indifference.

Sophia walked to the center of the room. "Naomi and Uncle Edward will be in need of a name for their future prodigy." Naomi's lips tightened to hide her smile at Sophia's in advertent use of "prodigy" in lieu of "progeny."

"In preparation for this party, I have researched some names."

All eyes skeptically regarded the mother-to-be.

Sophia immediately noted their disapproval and qualified her statement.

"You misunderstood! I am not making suggestions for their child's name. Besides, I have already used the three best ones," she giggled.

Well-acquainted with Sophia's sense of humor, all laughed with her—except Allison, who rolled her eyes and glanced to the bunting and mumbled, "Triplets and that wonderful husband."

"Did you say something?" Naomi asked.

"No, Mother."

Sophia glared at Allison and bit her bottom lip, but went on to explain, "All of us were given names at birth, but I venture to guess that most of you have no idea to their meaning. Am I right?"

A flurry of whispers and head shaking pleased the hostess.

"Very well, I have that information," she announced proudly. "As your hostess, I suppose you should know what my name means."

There was nodding in agreement.

She grinned ear-to-ear, "Sophia means wisdom." She looked to Hannah. "I guess my mother was accurately intuitive."

This inspired a wave of giggles. Sophia half-smiled—not quite sure if they agreed with her or were mocking her.

"What I discovered is that most of our names must have been initiated by our dear Lord's influence; they ironically seem nearly perfect for each and every one!" She pulled a paper from her pocket. "We will save our guest of honor for last, to insure some suspense. Livia—you are first."

She smiled shyly.

"Anyone care to take a go of it for the meaning of 'Livia'?" Hannah raised her hand.

"Mother?" Sophia pointed to her.

"Sweet, gentle and extremely patient...with my brother," Hannah laughed with the others.

"Very close, Mama. Actually, 'Livia" means peace and harmony—*exactly* what Uncle Hiram needs." Sophia grinned.

All were certain of that, but Livia wilted in her chair. Unbeknownst to those present, Hiram was not speaking to her—Rufus was still living in his home and calling her "Mummy." Peace and harmony did not describe the McDonnally household.

Allison raised a brow, having a history with

the difficult Hiram McDonnally. Sophia noted her response and spoke up, "Next, Allison."

Allison, Naomi's daughter, tried to demonstrate the appropriate enthusiasm, how ever wary she was of Sophia's findings.

"Who shall make a guess?" Sophia asked.

Harriet's hand shot up.

"Yes, Mrs. Dugan?"

"One who would be preferrin' the finer thin's." She offered a reprimanding glance toward the accused and a nod to her dear friend Eloise, whose son Guillaume was no longer engaged to the alleged "gold-digger."

"Near enough," Sophia verified quickly. "Allison means noble and exalted. Moving right along."

Allison's tongue pushed out a spot in her left cheek, while she squinted disapprovingly at the hostess abruptly changing the subject. Naomi half-smiled, noting the clash when Harriet begged, "What 'bout me?"

"Harriet. Anyone have an idea?" Sophia asked.

Harriet sat sternly, keenly eyeing the other guests. Her friend Eloise spoke up.

"Determined," she snickered.

"Very good, Mrs. Zigmann. Are you all prepared for this?"

The women nodded anxiously. Harriet leaned toward the hostess.

"Harriet means 'home ruler," Sophia reported.

Harriet slapped her thigh and burst out laughing. All joined in, until Harriet finally got control. "Aye, the good Lord had his hand in that choice, but me Joseph wouldna agree!"

When the roar died down, Eloise blurted out,

"What does mine mean?"

Sophia scanned her list. "Ah, yes. Who cares to make a guess?"

Naomi raised her hand.

"Guest of Honor?" inquired Sophia.

"Stable, like a rock. Dependable. Always there for you."

"Not exactly, but those attributes would certainly describe her meaning."

All waited intently.

"Eloise means 'famous warrior'."

Eloise nodded. "You have to be so, when in the master's employ and wife to Albert," she chuckled.

All seemed to be enjoying themselves and the fun continued.

"Aunt Beatrice, it is your turn," Sophia announced.

Allison, with a commanding, confident expression, raised her hand.

"Allison?" Sophia said casually.

"Grandmother's name should mean 'returning love.'"

Naomi patted her daughter's hand and smiled proudly.

"I am truly surprised, Allison, at your attempt," Sophia declared.

Allison's eyes narrowed.

"The name Beatrice means 'blessed voyager.'"

It was apparent by Beatrice's expression that she was quite content with the finding.

"Agnes Murray, you are next."

Agnes, a very shy girl, who did little socializing, was mortified at the very thought of being the focal point of the other guests. Seeing her discomfort, Sophia wasted no time for soliciting suggestions.

"As we all know, Agnes is betrothed to our poor injured postal carrier's son, Jake Kilvert, who is serving in the armed forces. Needless to say, she must be a woman of incredible strength and faith, at this time." All listened reverently, in utter silence.

"I am very pleased to verify that Agnes bears the name of 'one who is holy'. I think that we can unanimously agree that it is a well-suited name for Miss Murray." She turned her gaze to the holy one and offered a look of sympathy. All followed suit. Agnes gave a brief smile.

Sophia returned to study her list. "This one is a point of interest. I stumbled on Dagmar's name. I am sorry that Naomi's step-mother is not here to join us, but considering Nathan's return and his reclaiming the school..." she glanced to Naomi, Nathan's daughter. "I am sorry I did not mean to cast a dark shadow, over the party—Dagmar means 'day maid.' I thought that extraordinarily appropriate for a mercantile clerk."

Everyone seemed to agree. Allison covered her yawn. Sophia continued, as though she did not see it.

"Now it appears that two of our guests share part of their meaning. Those would be, my mother and Maryanne. That is, of course because 'Hannah' is a form of 'Ann'. Will someone take the challenge?"

Livia barely raised her arm and made a slight wave.

"Yes, Livia?"

"Loving'?"

"Excellent! Mary means 'beloved' and Hannah and Ann means 'to be favored by God.'"

A gust of 'ohs' filled the parlor.

"What about Mercedes?" Livia, now caught up in the enthusiasm, blurted out—then embarrassed, fell back into her chair.

"Ah yes..." Sophia scanned the list. "Here it is."

Mercy swallowed, praying it meant something acceptable and offered weakly, "Merciful?"

"Not for me Tavy," Harriet muttered, regarding Mercy and her adopted son's break up.

"*He* broke it off with me!" Mercy instantly responded.

Eloise glanced at her friend Harriet, and then looked away nervously, aware that her son Guillaume was now seeing Mercy. She dare not make eye contact with Allison, Guillaume's ex-fiancé.

"No, no. Anyone else?" Sophia broke up the banter.

"Wealthy one?" Allison blurted out in reference to Mercy's initial visit to Lochmoor Glen, charading as an impoverished gypsy.

"Not quite. Mercedes means wages or reward."

Allison immediately countered, "Reward? For whom?" she demanded.

A flurry of commentary began to take control.

"Ladies!" Sophia intervened. "We still have Trina, our returning resident."

"I would wager, 'innocent'!" Harriet bellowed with laughter. "Not wi' any help from yer man, Naomi!" All joined in the fun, as it was no secret that Edward had engaged Trina in an outrageous prank during the dinner party after he regained his memory.

Sophia barely controlling her own mirth and finally took control of the roaring, reminiscing crowd.

"Yes, yes, but ladies, listen! 'Tis true! Trina *does* mean 'innocent and pure'!"

The irony of the situation only added to the uproar.

After rehashing Edward's joke on the family, Sophia returned to the agenda. "Last but not least, guest of honor, Naomi, it is your turn."

All was quiet. Naomi was the backbone of the McDonnally clan and the village community. Suggestions flew from the crowd.

"Strong!"

"Sweet!"

"Sincere!"

"Bonnie!"

Sophia folded the paper and looked with admiration to her young "great aunt" Naomi.

"Indeed, Naomi, mother-again–to-be means 'pleasant and beautiful.'"

The response was a standing round of applause.

While Naomi blushed, Sophia invited the guests to partake in the refreshments while she fetched the tea.

"However, before I take a brief leave of you," she said, grinning like a Cheshire cat and pulling another piece of paper from her pocket for all to see, "I have the meaning of the names of our not so better halves!" She giggled.

The guests cheered at the news of learning the meaning of their counterpart's name. They then left their chairs to inspect the treats. To Sophia's dismay, the women, curious about Sophia's findings, quickly filled their china plates and returned to their seats, with no regard to her request for studying the photograph. Sophia made the rounds filling each cup, taking special care to move hastily out of range of Allison's slender form.

Sophia was overjoyed to find that her games were well received, and she loved being the center of attention. However, she was not so thrilled to see the vacant sandwich tray, and no one returning to check out the picture. She looked longingly at the five sandwiches piled on Harriet Dugan's plate and moved on with the teapot. How could she have miscalculated? Yes, she had taken care to honor the food rationing, but was certain that she had prepared enough. She was the only one to do without. She glanced around the circle of diners. Silly Allison had taken a ridiculous half of a sandwich.

You'll see. That tiny waist of yours will disappear after you have a baby. Sophia thought, watching Allison nibble at the crumb of a sandwich.

Harriet, of a rotund figure, was not the only one who had taken more than her allotted two. On returning the teapot to the table, Sophia made another devastating discovery; she cleared her throat and gulped at the cake plate, now empty. Livia was wrapping up the last piece in a napkin. Sophia knew that Livia was not saving it for herself; it was probably for her uncle as a reward for sitting with Kade.

Before Sophia had a chance to acknowledge her grief and pangs of hunger, Harriet exclaimed, "On with the show!"

The distracted hostess, trying to control her growling stomach, snapped back to the task at hand and withdrew the slip of paper.

"Before I begin, I might make mention of the all too familiar characteristics of the Scotsman."

Giggles filled the room.

"A true Scotsman is notably generous, but cantankerous. Chivalrous, but arrogant. He thrives on humor, but can be downright mean with his cutting remarks. And lastly, although he is hard-headed, he can be a sentimental fool at times. Note that I was referring to the Scots*man*."

Everyone laughed and applauded in agreement.

"Now, who shall we begin with, Naomi? Your choice."

"Edward, of course."

"Protector!" Allison offered.

Sophia glanced at the paper and then back to Allison. "Close, but not quite. 'Blessed guard.'"

"Not quite?" Allison objected. That was spot on. A guard is a protector!" she shot back.

"Not exactly." Sophia shook her head.

"Not exactly?" Allison's voice raised. "What is a guard, if not a protector?"

Naomi cut in, "I think that I should like that we move on to the next.

"What about my Albert?" Eloise asked. "Farmer?" Eloise giggled like a school girl.

"No, actually, 'noble and bright,'" Sophia grinned.

"Certainly, whatever you say," Eloise snickered dubiously.

"Let us hear the meaning for my Daniel. It must be sweet or genteel," Beatrice declared.

"No, but it is Hebrew for 'God is my judge.'"

Beatrice smiled. "I am certain that all will agree that Daniel will have no trouble entering the pearly gates when it is his time."

Sophia's eyes widened. "Speaking of Pearl, we forgot Pearl. I am so very sorry. I cannot apologize enough." Sophia had failed. All was going so well, and she had overlooked Naomi's quiet, sister-in law, Pearl, wife of Naomi's half-brother Henry and mother to Marvin and Conrad. Pearl was the one person who had travelled a great distance to attend.

All regarded Pearl with looks of concern.

Pearl smiled sweetly. "Pearl is 'a pearl', I suppose."

Sophia removed the other paper from her pocket and nervously unfolded it. "Here it is! Not just a pearl, but ever so 'precious.'"

Beatrice adored her son's choice for a wife and mother for his children. She left her chair and walked over to Pearl. She leaned down and hugged her. This one gesture nearly sent the entire group into tears. Sophia sniffled and returned the paper to her pocket.

"Back to the men folk," Harriet commanded. "What do ye hae to say about me Joseph?"

"Wise one?" Trina suggested.

Sophia ran her finger down the list. "Joseph— 'he will add.'"

"He will add?" Harriet responded, wrinkling her nose. "More laundry, more cookin', more cleanin' for me," she scoffed with a devilish glint in her eye. All laughed.

Sophia looked to Pearl. "Since I overlooked you in our first list, your Henry shall be next."

"I shan't even guess?" Pearl added.

"Prepare yourself, Mrs. Strickland."

"More like *Strictland,* of which he thinks he is king," Pearl giggled.

Sophia burst into laughter until the tears rolled. Her infectious laughter sent everyone rolling, unaware of the source of her amusement. Finally catching her breath, she spit out the words, "Henry means 'ruler of the household'!"

Pearl came up for air and chimed in, "That is what *he* would like to believe!"

"That goes for me Henry, as well!" Harriet joined in.

Sophia could not resist. "A show of hands— how many have husbands *or* sons who think they rule the roost?"

Still laughing, all of the married women raised their hands, some both hands.

Sophia felt a tinge of sympathy for Allison, without a beau or any prospects, who was not amused in the slightest.

"What 'bout me Bruce?" Maryanne insisted.

"Ah, yes, another one. Bruce is from the surname of Robert the Bruce, King of Scotland," Sophia reported.

"Aye, that will work!" Harriet exclaimed. "And what a kingdom! All lassies!"

Maryanne was not offended and remarked that Bruce often referred to his home as "his castle." All nodded in solidarity.

Sophia looked at Livia solemnly, then could not help but smiling as she said, "Uh oh, Uncle Hiram." A hush fell over the group. Then a flood of adjectives came forth:

"Handsome!" Trina called out.

"Fickle!" Allison countered.

"Royalty!" Maryanne offered.

"Stubborn!" Livia inadvertently shouted.

"Room destroyer" Eloise yelled, jumping from her chair and then quickly sat down, blushing from her harsh, but accurate choice—having been responsible for cleaning up the aftermath of his countless explosions of temper.

"Actually, 'Hiram' has two meanings. One highest in rank and the other exalted brother." Sophia turned to her mother, Hiram's twin.

Hannah raised a brow and then gave a genuine smile. "Sophia, what about Oscar?"

"Oscar—'divine spear.'"

Hannah forced a smile. She did not like the association of Oscar with a weapon. He had just come back into her life. She had held her breath in hopes that he would not put on a uniform, Oscar being too old to go to the front, in her opinion.

Naomi raised her hand, curious about her one time poetry partner. "And Guillaume?"

Allison looked away to the window while Mercy listened intently.

"Guillaume means resolute protector," Sophia said respectfully.

Mercy sat back, wearing an expression of pure satisfaction. With a trace of regret, Allison focused on the napkin that she folded in her lap; she had ended her engagement with Guillaume, but with no argument on his part.

Livia casually raised her hand. "What about Mr. Merriman, the schoolmaster?" she asked nonchalantly, knowing Hiram would have had a conniption had he known that she had inquired about his nemesis.

"Joel. Hmm?" Sophia panicked. Had she included him? "Ah, yes, strong-willed."

He needed to be, working in Hiram's home, Livia thought.

In scrutinizing the list, Jake's name had jumped out at her. She had overlooked it. She had to do something quickly.

"Other than Rahzie, I have saved the honored for last—to leave you with a high note. The honorable, Mr. Jacob Kilvert. There would probably be a different suggestion from each of you, but one should stand out in your mind. Jake was the first native of Lochmoor Glen to go off to war. Courageous, is the word I would choose, but his name appropriately means 'may God protect,'" Sophia explained. All applauded; Agnes cried, which tugged on the heartstrings of the others.

After a few minutes of pulling themselves together, the hostess wrapped things up.

"I think that I can safely say that although we spoke of our male companions in jest, none of us could imagine life without them. My husband's name is Rahzvon Manstrong. Some may feel his middle name was a rather...excessive choice. It was his mother's wish for him to be just that. He is. And for that, I am thankful—especially with triplets. His first name is Gisaleon and from what I could translate, it means 'messenger of good news.'"

At that moment, Rahzvon stepped into the parlor.

Sophia stared awestruck at Rahzvon's timely arrival. Apparently, so did Allison, as she nearly left her chair. Sophia was well aware that many, including Allison, considered Rahzvon to be every woman's dream for the perfect partner: handsome, strong, passionate, good father and faithful husband.

He held up his hand clutching a tattered, stained envelope. "Miss Murray, this is for you, from a Mr. Jacob Kilvert."

The women swooned at the miraculous delivery by the "messenger of good news," hoping it was just that.

Agnes stood up. Her hand trembled as she withdrew it from Rahzvon's.

Sophia immediately intervened, "Please, Agnes, go upstairs. There you can have some privacy."

"Thank ye, Mum." She stared at the treasure and slowly moved up the stairs.

Sophia turned to the now silent congregation.

"Shall we celebrate with the passing out of the party favors...uh one per guest, if you please."

Agnes went to the end of the hall and sat on the little bench beneath the window. She ran her finger under the envelope flap and removed Jake's letter.

Dearest Bonnie Lassie,

I miss you so very much and have so little time to write. I have a new trench mate—wee MacKenzie. No relation to Naomi or that cur Nathan. She is a dog. A mighty fine rat terrier. The wee lass is a bloody grand ratter and companion. Please excuse me language, love, but she is the blessing I'd been praying for. Before she arrived, the rats were intolerable. I no longer need to keep me face covered when I get a bit of sleep to protect it from the vermin. I shared me cheese with her and spared her a few bites of dried vegetables. Me bread is stale now and the tea water is tainted from the petrol can, but bearable. Forgive me for saying, but the lice are everywhere. Running a candle flame down our uniform seams gives some relief.

The war cannot end soon enough. 'Tis difficult to keep track of time here. Tell the folks I will write soon.

My bonnie Agnes, I leave you with my everlasting love and gratitude for your letters. Me mates all had a good laugh over the Mr. Peanut that you wrote about. We voted that he should don a helmet and a rifle instead of a top hat and cane!

I dream of you whenever I get a wee chance to close me eyes.

Soon we will begin our life together,
All my love, Jake

Agnes dropped the letter into her lap, bit her bottom lip and placed the missive back in the envelope. She would not cry. She could not cry. She would not be afraid. He would be coming safely home to her.

Chapter III

"Behind Bars"

"Till, one day, crawling seemed suspect,
He gripped the air and stood erect
And splendid
With immortal rage,
He entered on man's heritage."

—Stephen Vincent Benet

The successful tea was the subject of conversation for months to come. Knowledge of the plethora of meanings that Sophia provided also made their way into many family discussions. Sophia's hopes for more input on the photograph were dashed, but she was pleased with her guests' response. She had successfully hosted a grand tea party. Her true reward was the dinner afterward with her husband—his treat—or so she believed. The company was grand, but the idea of a meal that she did not need to prepare or cleanup afterward, ranked superb.

Sophia dabbed her mouth with her napkin.

"Now, how is it that Uncle Hiram agreed to tend to the children, this evening? I cannot imagine him volunteering. He is not alone, is he?"

"No, Marvel and Wilmoth Wheaton are giving him a hand. Phia, it was purely a stroke of good fortune. Hiram was naturally pleased to see our brood, but immediately showed concern at the fact that I came without you."

"Surely he knew about the tea."

"Yes, he knew." Rahzvon took a last bite of potato. "He was enjoying a peaceful afternoon, while Kade was asleep in the nursery."

"And?"

He crinkled his brow. "After I finished my route, I returned to your uncle's. I am not sure exactly how it all came about, but someone came up with the idea—a challenge of sorts, as to who could get their baby to fall asleep first. Not Kade, but two out of three of ours—Ruthia and Von."

Sophia tossed her napkin on the table. "You were laying odds down on my precious babies?"

"It is not as bad as it seems. Phia, we were

bored and Ruthia was throwing one of her tantrums."

"It was not a tantrum. She was missing me."

"Whatever the reason, she was out of control."

"Uncle Hiram took her, of course."

"Yes, yes, he did. Exactly as I had hoped."

"And Zanya? She did not make a peep."

He nodded. "Not a peep. She was good as gold—playing with her fingers and toes. I wish that I could say the same or our son."

"So who won?"

"I did. Hiram thought he had it wrapped up, taking Ruthia. The two of us paced up and down that parlor; he with Ruthia, me with Von, and Zanya asleep in the crib. Kade was still asleep; I cannot imagine how, as Von was wailing up a storm. I wish you could have seen the smug look on Hiram's face because Ruthia just smiled, seemingly fascinated with his black curls."

"That is because she loves playing with my ringlets."

He took a sip of water. "Finally, Von started to drift off and Ruthia was playing with Hiram's beard. That's the crux of it. He lost—I won."

"And what were the stakes? I hope you did not give away one of our children."

"Don't be silly. If I lost, I would mend the back fence along Margaret's Lane; if he lost he had to sit with our three and pay for our supper," he said triumphantly.

"You are awful, Mr. Sierzik. You knew all along that Ruthia was the only one of the three who had a three hour nap this morning."

"Privileged information, my love."

"Rahzie, we need to finish our afters and

rescue them."

"Rescue Hiram and the Wheaton girls or our babies?" he laughed.

"All of them. But especially the babies. It is time to feed them!"

Unfortunately, for Hiram, Maryanne retrieved her daughters, Marvel and Wilmoth, directly after the tea, assuring Hiram that Livia, Hannah, and Eloise would be returning shortly. However, Maryanne was not aware that the three women had decided to visit Mrs. Stewart and deliver her party favor and piece of cake. Maryanne's cart had barely left the drive before Zanya and her brother had wakened. Naturally, their excruciating vocal objections to the absence of their mother wakened Kade.

When the parents returned, Miles opened the door, bouncing Vonmanstrong with tear stained cheeks. "Thank the Lord! Master, they are here!" Miles declared.

Sophia immediately rescued her son and rushed into the parlor.

"Great Scott, Uncle Hiram! What has happened?" She glanced around the room and down at Hiram's right leg, wrapped in Kade's trembling arms. The little boy looked truly the part of the abandoned orphan.

Before Hiram had a chance to reply, Sophia noted Rahzvon picking up Zanya, who was whimpering pathetically. Sophia announced, "Never mind, I am going to the study to feed Von. I will be back in a few minutes to feed the girls."

Rahzvon cuddled Zanya. "My poor girl, you

seldom ever cry. Did he ignore you? Were you lonely or afraid?" he asked softly.

"See here, Mr. Sierzik! This was your idea! You made the terms of the bet."

Rahzvon cradled Zanya in his arms where she snuggled down peacefully. "You should not have agreed to terms that you could not keep," he replied smugly.

"How was I to know that the Wheaton girls were going to up and leave me?" he shouted above Ruthia's blaring screams for her mother.

Miles flew in through the archway.

"Mrs. Sierzik says that you two need to pipe down. You are scaring the infants."

Miles had barely delivered his message when Livia entered, accompanied by the notorious Rufus, who immediately voiced his opinion.

"Mr. Donnally, you look disgustin'!" He wrinkled up his nose and walked over to the wet, stained master. "Mummy, he stinks, too!"

Kade broke free from Hiram's trousers and toddled over to his mother, relieved to see her comforting face.

"Livy, get Rufus out of here, or I shall not be responsible for what happens, next!"

She scooped up Kade, snatched Rufus's hand and rushed them from the room. Rahzvon leaped at the opportunity.

"He was right, Hiram, you smell atrocious."

"Not another word, Sierzik. Not *one*."

Once again, shielded by his precious daughter, Rahzvon took the risk.

"*Mummy*? I guess you and Livia *are* adopting Rufus." He broke into laughter and moved quickly to the opposite end of the room.

***

The next day grew dark while Rahzvon returned to the peace of his postal route and his final deliveries. He left a few posts for the Stewarts and made his final stop at the Wheaton farm. He approached the dilapidated house where little Jeanie stood in the yard. She appeared to be instructing three ducks, standing attentively at her feet.

"Good afternoon, Jeanie. Are you still my girl?" he asked, approaching her and extending his hand with a single envelope.

"Hello, sir. I am dreadfully sorry, but I am not," she said sincerely.

"You are not?" he said in a tone of slight disappointment. "Have I been replaced?"

"Me heart belongs to anoth'r."

"A duck?"

"Nay." Jeanie giggled. "One wi' no wife, nor a parcel o' bairns."

"Oh..." Rahzvon dropped his head trying to remain serious and look truly depressed. Finally, he raised his head. "Master Marvin Strickland?"

"Aye, sir." Her expression transformed to one of sheer delight. "He came to visit, thanks to yer wife."

"Ah, yes, his mother Pearl was invited to Phia's tea party."

He offered the envelope to her. "Could you please give this to your mother?"

"Nay, sir. So sorry, but me ducks are in need o' their daily bath. Can ye not see their dirty feathers?"

He withdrew his hand and raised a brow. "Yes, filthy. Do they have names?"

She giggled again. "Ev'rybody is named." She pointed to the smallest bird. "This wee lassie is Shirley. This one is Goodness and the big round one is named for Miss Stockdale."

"Miss Stockdale, eh?"

"Aye, Mama says she is a fine lady."

"That she is."

"We must go, now. Good-bye, sir. Come along," she called to her muddy friends.

Rahzvon watched the little girl's faded blue ribbons floating over her shoulders while she skipped towards the pond; the three waddled behind her without hesitation.

Rahzvon chuckled to himself, "Shirley, Goodness, and Mercy shall follow her for the rest of the days of her life." He mounted up. "Clever girl—fickle, but clever. And to think that I have two...three, with Phia."

The autumn months presented a series of new concerns for the Sierzik family; their three "clever" children were self-propelled by crawling power. The triplets had developed a keen interest in investigating their somewhat limited surroundings. Their overwhelmed parents' discussion of their children's incredible mobility, escalated one October morning. Rahzvon and Sophia sat across from each other with their progeny lost in a sea of wooden toys and pots and pans below them.

"What are you going to do about it?" Sophia said in short temper.

"What am *I* going to do? You do not see Zanya and Von climbing the couch like a pair of monkeys."

"It shan't be long before they do. Ruthia

cannot be blamed for being intellectually advanced like her mother."

"*That* is not Ruthia's problem—she thrives on attention, *like* her mother. Every time I order her to get down, she turns around and grins at me."

"That is because she wants you to be proud of her climbing abilities."

"No she doesn't. She knows that I am worried about her and that I will drop everything to rescue her from injuring herself."

He squinted at the mischievous daughter. She removed the leg of the wooden horse from her mouth and smiled at her father. He rolled his eyes and tried desperately to hide a returning smile from the little imp who never failed to touch his heart—not at all *unlike* her mother.

Sophia interrupted the silent exchange. "We are going to have to move the divan elsewhere."

"Move the couch? Where?"

"To the attic, for now. The barn is too damp," she said, puffing up a pillow and placing it in the corner behind her.

"The attic?" he objected.

"Are you willing to sacrifice the safety of all three of your children?"

"Where are *you* going to sit?" he shot back.

"In that rocking chair that you are enjoying, at present. It *is* for rocking the children. You will have to bring in one of the dining room chairs for yourself. It can be easily returned to the table when you are not sitting in it—so as not to jeopardize Ruthia's well-being."

He leaned back in the rocker.

"Phia. Look at this place. It is a disaster. It looks like the local jail—bars on the windows, a gate across the hearth, and these tables with nothing on them—not even a copy of *The Motor World*! Why leave *them* in here? They serve no purpose, whatsoever."

"That is completely inaccurate. I often put blankets over the tables to make little tents for the children."

Rahzvon flew from the chair. "I told you—no more blankets in here! Our son nearly smothered, wound up in one!"

"Stop yelling at me! I know, I know! I do not make tents for them *anymore*! Besides they like to walk around them holding on to the edges."

"They are going to pull them over on top of themselves—I told you that!"

"Stop yelling!"

"I am not yelling! You are! I cannot live like this! No one does."

"How do you know?"

"The Wheatons have six daughters and never put up barriers like a cell. They discipline their children."

"What are you instigating?"

"I am *insinuating* that we should not have to turn our home into a stall. If you used the word 'no' we would not be having this problem."

"Ah! No, no, no! I am not listening to you and your gibberish anymore! This is equally your responsibility! So do the one thing to help matters! Take it to the attic! I am going to the kitchen to prepare healthy meals for my three lovely children!" She stomped out.

"Who is going to tend to your three lovely children, if I am supposed to be heaving the blasted couch up to the attic?" he called after her.

The rap at the door sent Sophia scrambling through an obstacle course of toys in the hall. She opened the door to see the not-so-jovial faces of Hiram, Livia and Rufus. Hiram lowered Kade to the floor; who ran to join the children in the parlor.

Livia forced a smile and offered Sophia a brown parcel. "Kade outgrew these—they are for Von."

The dissonance in the family was quite apparent. The visit was brief with very little discussion. After bidding the McDonnally crew farewell, Sophia turned to Rahzvon.

"It is Rufus—he is the problem. Would you consider—"

"Absolutely not, Phia. We cannot even handle these three."

Rufus's well-being was not only on Sophia's mind. In the following months after his meeting with Rufus at the Brachney Hall pond, Tavy became reserved and isolated. He spent little time with anyone, including Joseph and Harriet. He performed his chores, but kept to himself in the evening hours—often just walking the moors or fishing.

Early one morning after those silent months, he slammed his fist down on the breakfast table.

"I canna do this!"

"Do what, son?" Joseph asked.

"Forgive me. But I hae n' other choice."

He left the cottage.

Tavy's footsteps led him to the entrance of the McDonnally mansion where he met Livia who was exiting.

"Good morning, Henry."

"Mornin', mum. Do ye hae time to speak wi' me?"

"Certainly, come on in."

"This will take but a minute."

She ushered him to the vacant parlor. "Please, have a seat. What is it, Henry?"

"Please, be honest wi' me, Miss Nichols—not that ye wouldn't."

"I will," she mumbled fearfully, not knowing what he was about to ask.

"Is the young laddie happy here in yer home, wi' ye and Hiram?"

"Kade?"

"Nay—Rufus."

Livia let out a sigh. "I am trying to make it work but..."

"Hiram doesna approve."

She shook her head with dismay.

"Mum, I want to raise Rufus."

"But Henry—"

"I am aware I am not a proper family—only a pa...but I understand the lad. We are cut from the same cloth. I canna offer him the life or opportunities o' the McDonnallys, but I hae adequate income."

Livia took her seat next to him. "I do not know what to say."

"It would be best for yer home."

"Henry, I cannot ask you to do such a charitable deed. It would change your life, forever."

"Aye, it would—for the better."

"Have you spoken to Harriet and Joseph about this?"

"It doesna matter."

"Henry, you cannot take Rufus out of pity. You will come to resent him."

"Nay, I need the laddie and he needs me. I would regret it, if I didn't. I hae given it a great deal o' thought."

"You really do want him."

"Aye, if he wants the same."

"But when? It is just so sudden."

"Now."

Her eyes widened and jaw dropped. She was silent for a moment and then explained, "I suppose that there really is no need to discuss this with Hiram...Wait here, please. I will speak with Rufus. He is in the kitchen with Eloise."

Tavy paced around the room, noting the fine furnishings, the portraits of the McDonnallys adorning the walls. He would be taking Rufus away from all of this, and to what? The Dugan home? Ma Dugan had less tolerance for Rufus than Hiram. Maybe he was making a mistake—but it was too late, now.

All remorse dissipated when Rufus appeared in the archway. He ran to Tavy and hugged his waist, seemingly aware that his wish to become a part of Livia's life was moot.

"Come, Rufus, we need to get back home for chores."

Knowing Tavy's tremendous desire to raise Rufus, the Dugans accepted his decision. Rufus worked with Tavy, doing his best to follow orders. After a couple hours of cleaning the barn and harvesting the south field, the two entered the Dugan cottage in answer to Harriet's dinner bell.

"Wash yer hands and sit down, lads."
"Rufus, how de ye like yer taties?"
He made no hesitation to reply.

*"Yokie Pokie, Yankie, fun,
how do ye like yer taties done?
First in brandy, then in rum."*

Rufus then shouted,
"That's how I like me taties done!"

Harriet glared at Tavy. "Henry McTavish, did ye teach him that?"

The guilty party lowered his head and continued eating.

When they finished their meal, Tavy addressed Joseph, the gout ridden patient, "How are ye feelin' Pa?"

"Better, today."

Rufus walked over to Joseph and glared down at the effected big toe. His eyes widened and reached down and touched it.

"Agh!" Joseph wailed. "Get him out o' here!"

"Sorry, Pa!" Tavy quickly escorted the curious boy outside, toward the barn.

"Carrot Top, how would ye like to take a wee journey wi' me? I think we are both due for a holiday." His thoughts returned to his break up with Mercy.

"Where are we goin'?"

"To Clovelly."

"Where is that?"

"Far south—in England. 'Tis many miles from here."

"Who is in Clov..."

"Clovelly. Not who—what. A Christmas gift for Ma Dugan from Pa."

"Must be special."

"Aye, verra. While we are there, I need to be checkin' out a schooner that me mate gave me— the *Kinney May*. Knowin' Dobby Bowes, it probably willna be worth the time to see it. What do ye think? We'll be leavin' right after the McDonnally weddin'."

Rufus glanced over his shoulder toward the window where Ma could be seen ranting silently.

"Tavy, I think a man needs to get away from his troubles. I'll join ye."

Livia sat in the study going over the wedding plans. She glanced up to see Kade methodically walking along the bookcase, touching each of the bindings of the volumes on the lower shelf, with his tiny index finger. Hiram sat, quietly engrossed in his paperwork at his desk. Peace reigned. She thought back to Tavy's visit. Rufus's leaving the McDonnally estate was bittersweet for her. Although she was consumed with guilt for failing Rufus, she was equally relieved that the wall between her and Hiram had crumbled away. She put it behind her and focused on the upcoming wedding and being a good mother to Kade.

Chapter IV

"Wedded Bliss"

"Hear the mellow wedding bells—
Golden Bells!
What a world of happiness their
Harmony foretells!
Through the balmy air of night
How they ring out their delight!"

—Edgar Allan Poe

Guillaume held the door open to the Zigmann cottage.

"Come on in for a while, Mercy. Mother and Father are visiting with Beatrice and Daniel."

Mercy nodded and led the way.

"Guillaume, is it not a bit awkward?"

"What?"

"Your mother visiting with Daniel and Beatrice."

"Mother's and Daniel's relationship is merely history—like Allison's and mine. Here, take this chair." He offered an overstuffed chair by the fireplace. "It is the best in the house."

"Thank you." She sat down and sighed. "What a day to remember."

"That it is," he said, pulling the rocking chair up next to her.

"But they are finally married—Mr. and Mrs. Hiram McDonnally."

"Indeed they are and after surviving today, I feel confident that they can take on anything that life throws at them."

Mercy crossed her ankles. "The food was delicious."

"It was. Mother outdid herself. What an array."

"I have to ask, Guillaume, is it a Scottish custom to offer only spoons. It was a bit awkward. I felt like a small child."

"No, absolutely not. In fact, Mother was fit to be tied. She had told Father to bring the silver from the table. The spoons, the last she had polished had still been left out. So, he brought *only* the spoons."

"Typical man." She glanced at his

disapproving grin and apologized. She gave a little laugh. "There were a few bites that I had to chase around the plate."

"'Twas strange eating the cake with a spoon," he agreed.

"The cake—yes, what happened to the top tier? Livia so wanted a tiered cake."

"You missed that episode? It was the bird."

"Not that bird that was dive bombing everyone while we were waiting for the minister?" Her eyes widened.

"'Tis the very one. It made a crash landing into the top tier. Harriet discreetly removed the layer."

"Oh, no." She shook her head.

"It may have been avoided if Reverend Briscoll had not been forty-five minutes late."

"I overheard Mr. Wheaton say that his buggy wheel fell off. He could have been killed and then Hiram and Livia would still be engaged."

"Mercy, there were a few times, today, well several times, that I felt it may have been better if they *had* postponed it."

"True. I never witnessed so much chaos on one given day."

"Neither have I and that is quite a feat having lived several years in Lochmoor Glen."

"I heard Harriet say that the bride and groom passed the Stewart's lost pig on the way to the village. According to the belief, their bad luck could be foregone, if they returned to the mansion and restarted the journey to the church. They did, but I am not sure how successful it was…poor Livia, forgetting her vows and it was her idea to compose her own."

"Better she than Hiram. He would have never lived it down."

Mercy leaned back. "They did make a handsome couple. Overall, it was a beautiful ceremony."

"Except for Livia's wedding gown."

"Guillaume, I cannot tell you how many times that I mentioned that nail sticking up in the aisle."

"Angus was planning to remove it last week, but he took sick."

"Any simpleton could have fixed it with one good stroke of a hammer. I felt so sorry for her, leaving half of that delicate imported lace train behind her."

"She handled it well—like nothing happened. *Oh*, but the pinning." He shook his head. "I cannot believe that Hannah actually stuck the bride with the clan badge when pinning the sash."

"Unfortunate for both parties. Livia had to still be in pain from Kade's dropping the good luck horseshoe on her foot... I have to commend you, Guillaume for your quick response to take the initiative to light the lamps when the storm blew in. It got so dark so quickly. I will admit that I had a few flashing memories of the twister with Sophia."

"Thanks, but I felt terrible about bumping Joseph's sore toe."

"So did everyone else. The acoustics are incredible in that church. That bellow nearly broke my eardrums. Of course, it had to turn pitch black right when Edward handed Hiram the ring."

"Mercy, I have had some truly embarrassing moments, but I cannot imagine how Edward felt when that ring went rolling under the pews."

"Yes, and then there was that quarrel between Rufus and Marvin. All I heard was that they were fighting over the ring and each wanted it for Jeanie Wheaton."

"Popular, little lassie. Poor Pearl had to intervene and recover the ring." Guillaume rocked a little.

It was quiet for a few minutes.

"Too bad about the flowers," Mercy mumbled.

"Someone will pay for that error in judgment, if I know Hiram."

"Imagine paying all that money to import flowers and then being delivered two hours late, smack in the middle of the ceremony."

Guillaume leaned forward. "What's worse was Gantwell's entry. What an uproar! A dog at the ceremony!"

"I guess we cannot hold the delivery man accountable for letting the dog in."

Guillaume started to laugh and then held back.

"Sir, it is not proper to make fun at another's expense," she said, trying not to smile.

"But did you see Hiram's stocking? He adores that dog, but I thought he was going to kill her when she wouldn't let go!"

Mercy covered the forbidden smile with her hand. "I still think that he looked quite handsome in his kilt, tattered stocking and all."

"Oh, I do not know. Wearing Edward's jacket was the straw that broke the camel's back."

"They made the best of an unexpected situation. I think he looked fine."

"*Unexpected* situation, Mercy? It was disgusting!"

"What other choice did Hiram have? That thunder crash scared Ruthia. She was screaming and reaching for him. How was he to know that she was ill?"

"But taking the child during the ceremony?"

"He knew that he could calm her quickly," she explained.

"Oh, she was calmed all right. She stopped crying long enough to lose her breakfast all down the front of him, and then Kade threw a tantrum because he was jealous of Hiram holding Ruthia."

"You are making too much out of it. It was all resolved very quickly by the exchange of jackets. Beatrice took Hiram's out...but I am still confused about the stench in the church."

"Oh, that. Before the ceremony, when my father delivered the food to the church he found that some wretched culprit had turned a pony lose in there."

"Who would do such a thing?"

"Some suspect Rufus. He had a motive, being jealous of Hiram."

"Why didn't your father clean it up?"

"He tried, but did not have much time. I guess he missed a pile."

The two sat silently recollecting the numerous mishaps.

Mercy remembered, "Poor Mrs. Stewart, I thought that she would never stop coughing. It surprised the entire congregation when Rufus presented her with a glass of water."

"Ah, Tavy probably planned to curb the suspicions of Rufus being responsible for the loose pony. Besides, Mrs. Stewart was afraid to drink it from the hand of that scallywag."

Mercy placed her hand on her stomach. "I ate entirely too much."

"Me, too. I am stuffed. I need to cut back."

"Guillaume Zigmann you are a beanpole. You will never need to watch your waistline...What happened to the music after the ceremony?"

"Gantwell. It was Hiram's fault. Remember when he put Gantwell out and she kept howling?"

"Yes. He brought her in and tied her to the pew with the aisle cord."

"A little too close in proximity to Joseph's bagpipes, Mercy. They do not carry a tune with holes in the bag."

She wrinkled up her nose at the thought. "How angry was Joseph?"

"After my hitting his toe, his patience had reached its limit. I was there when he gave the groom a piece of his mind. Naturally, Hiram offered to buy him a new set."

"Good."

"Not really. Those pipes were handed down three generations."

"Hmm."

Guillaume rocked again. "The Wheaton girls looked especially nice."

"Yes, Maryanne made all of their matching dresses from a bolt of fabric from Mrs. Stewart. Did you see that duckling Jeanie was harboring under her cape?" Mercy giggled.

"Who did not? I thought Maryanne was going to die from exhaustion trying desperately to keep Bruce from seeing it... The sword presentation went well—Hiram did not stab Livia," he laughed.

"The sword is handed down to the first born son," Mercy noted. "I wonder how Kade will feel about that…if they have another son."

"Very insightful. I never considered it." He reached up and stretched. "The bride's cog was tasty," he said, referring to the honorary drink which is served in the half barrel with handles.

"A bit too much whiskey," she added.

"I am nearly certain that Angus had a hand in that." They both laughed.

Guillaume stared at Mercy. "If I ever marry, I shan't submit myself to the torture and humiliation of a formal wedding."

"I hope that your future wife agrees."

"She had better. Or she shan't be my bride."

"Funny, how Hiram and Livia chose not to partake in the traditional bride and groom activities, the night before, because they wanted to keep it *simple*."

"They made up for it, today."

"Guillaume, did you see Hiram and Livia's faces before we left the church?" she asked, smiling.

"That is all I probably care to remember about today."

"They were so happy. You could see their love for one another radiating all about them, like two interlinked haloes."

Guillaume stared at her, nodded and leaned back in the rocker.

Tavy and his new sidekick, Rufus, headed toward the village mercantile to pick up supplies for their journey to Clovelly. Finally, Rufus's curiosity got the best of him.

"What gift do they have in Clovelly that Pa Dukan canna buy here? Jewels?"

"Nay, a wee donkey."

"Ma Dukan wants a *donkey*?" Rufus could not imagine it.

"I am not certain o' that, but Pa thinks that she needs one."

"Why?"

"They are always squabblin' over the use of Jock, so Pa wants another mule."

"Then why are we fetchin' a donkey?"

"Because he wants more mules."

Tavy stopped the cart at the mercantile and studied the confused boy's expression. "I will explain later. Out ye go."

Tavy and Rufus entered the store. Rufus eyed every item displayed on the shelves. Dagmar MacKenzie had left the shop management to a young man, who consequently had been recently called away for a funeral of a fallen relative. He had also notified her that he would not be returning. Meanwhile, Mrs. Kilvert had taken charge

"Afternoon, Tavy!"

"Afternoon, Mrs. Kilvert. Any word from Jake?"

"Aye, Rahzvon delivered a post only yesterday. He is well," she sniffled.

"When ye write, tell him I send me best."

"Thank ye, Tavy," she dabbed her eyes.

Mrs. Kilvert kept a sharp eye on Rufus while Tavy stacked his supplies on the counter. Tavy put two thermoses on the counter and turned to see Rufus peering through a spyglass, which he was directing out the window.

"Need somethin' Rufus?" Tavy asked.

"Nay," he said solemnly and placed the

spyglass back on the shelf.

"'Tis everythin'?" Mrs. Kilvert asked.

"Nay, would ye hae a wee pair o' jeans for me young friend?"

"Aye, a new shipment came in yesterday."

She pulled a pair from a box on the shelf behind her.

"Here, these should fit."

"Thank ye," Tavy said, removing his money pouch from his pocket.

Mrs. Kilvert tallied up the purchases and placed them in a burlap bag with Tavy's assistance. He was paying her when Trina Dunmore walked into the store. Mrs. Kilvert deposited the payment, thanked him, and asked Trina if she needed assistance. Trina declined the offer and Mrs. Kilvert returned to feather dusting the china.

Chapter V

"Meeting Her Match"

"An argument is like a country road,
you never know where it is going to lead."

—Anonymous

"Hello, Henry."

"Trina, 'tis good to see ye," Tavy said, tying the bag closed.

"I was surprised that the first time that I saw you was at the wedding. Lochmoor Glen is *not* Paris," she teased, referring to the diminutive size of the village

"I have been busy o' late."

"Picking up supplies for the Dugans?"

"Nay, I have an errand to run for Pa. We are goin' to Clovelly."

"*We?* Have you reconciled with Miss Stockdale?"

"I was referrin' to me new mate, Rufus." He pointed to the small boy studying a magnifying lens and holding it up to a book directly in line with a stream of sunlight. Tavy shot past her and snatched it from the boy as the page began to smoke. He laid it back on the counter.

"Aye, we are goin' to fetch a donkey!" Rufus chimed in.

Trina said in a hushed tone, "Sorry to hear about you and Mercy, Henry."

"Are ye?"

"Well yes...broken relationships are always a sad event."

"Are they?" he asked, picking up the sack. "Mercy and I are from different worlds. We couldna make a go o' it... Come along, Carrot Top." He waved at Trina.

She watched the two load the cart and climb in.

"Who is the boy, Mrs. Kilvert?"

"An orphaned lad; orphaned only recently."

Trina wandered over to the fabric table. She

picked up a swatch of a floral periwinkle. "Mercy, from a different world—one of wealth," she mumbled."

"Do ye need some help, Miss Dunmore?"

"No, no thank you." *Nothing with which you can help me.*

Just then Tavy reentered the store alone and made an additional purchase. He walked over to Trina.

"Maybe I'll be seein' ye, when we return."

"Yes, yes, I will look forward to it."

"Will ye?" he asked, grinning.

She hesitated and nodded. Tavy sauntered out the door.

Allison was sitting in the drawing room, scanning the articles in the *Lady's Realm* when Joel Merriman, the schoolmaster arrived. He waited impatiently in the corridor, reviewing the contents of his script to present to the enchanting Miss O'Connor. He had seen her on only a few occasions, but found her appearance, especially at the wedding, nothing less than enticing. Being alone and Lochmoor Glen's newest resident, he naturally received invitations from the others to dine with them. Tonight he was dining with the occupants of Brachney Hall. Originally, Naomi had added Hiram and Livia to the guest list, but Livia declined, explaining that Joel would probably appreciate a few hours away from McDonnally Manor and Hiram.

Naomi was busy pinning up the last strands of her hair before the she went to welcome her guest, when their house guest, Trina, tapped on the doorjamb of the master bedroom.

"Naomi?"

"Yes, Trina?"

"Might I ask who shall be attending tonight?"

"The four of us and Mr. Merriman. Neither of the other two eligible bachelors, Guillaume and Mr. McTavish will be coming—if you are wondering," Naomi snickered.

Trina glanced away nervously, rolled her eyes, and grinned, not surprised that she could not conceal her thoughts from the omniscient Naomi. "Very well, then, please tell me about Joel. Allison never mentioned him."

Naomi left the bench of the dressing table. "He is young, and dashing. I am sure you noticed that when you met him at the wedding. He is very intelligent, but a bit shy—except with Livia."

"*Livia?*"

"Yes, they have an unknown history—to Hiram's dismay. They do work quite well together; also to Hiram's dismay."

"I wonder why Allison never said anything about him."

"I have no information in that regard, but you can judge for yourself. Let us go downstairs."

Allison called to them, "I thought that you two were never coming down. Jules says that the schoolmaster is waiting in the hall," she added in passing while flipping through the pages of *Photoplay*.

"You left him in the hall?" Naomi asked in disbelief.

"I did not. Jules did."

"Why did you not ask him to join you? He must think us to be so awfully rude."

"Oh, Mother, he is *only* the schoolmaster."

Trina exchanged a disturbed glance with Naomi. Naomi hustled in to greet him and quickly extended her apologies. She led him into the drawing room.

"Trina, you remember Mr. Merriman from the wedding."

"Hello, Joel."

"Good evening, Miss...Dunmore."

"You may call me Trina."

"My pleasure." He reached for her hand under the scrutiny of Allison's discreet gaze. His focus immediately shifted from her hand to rest on the countenance of the resigned Miss O'Connor.

"Good evening, Miss O'Connor."

She casually left her seat, glanced at him and nodded. "Mr. Merriman."

Trina withdrew her hand from his and stared curiously at her aloof friend. Jules stepped in from the hall.

"The meal is ready to be served."

Confused by her daughter's rude behavior, Naomi suggested, "Joel, if you could please escort Miss Dunmore into the dining room. We will be there directly."

Joel took Trina's arm and they followed Jules. Naomi took hold of her daughter's forearm.

"What is the matter with you, tonight, Allison?"

"Whatever do you mean, Mother?" she asked, avoiding any eye contact.

"Your negative attitude towards Mr. Merriman."

"I have no attitude concerning Mr. Merriman. Now, shall we join father in the dining room?"

Naomi rolled her eyes and led the way to

where Jules was waiting to seat them. Edward sat at the head of the table and Naomi sat across from him. Trina was seated next to Joel—Allison directly across from him. Edward initiated the conversation while the first course was served.

"Have you adapted to village life, Mr. Merriman?"

"*Joel*, please. Yes, very well, thank you—despite the relocation of the school—unexpected as it was. The delayed shipment of supplies is trickling in; the new primers should be arriving shortly." He looked to Allison. "I noted your interest in reading, Miss O'Connor."

She laid her spoon down. "Does not everyone read?" she replied without hesitation.

He laughed, albeit uncomfortably, at the cutting remark and replied, "Not everyone...or I would be without employment."

Edward glanced at Naomi who forced a brief laugh to humor their targeted guest.

"Mr.—Joel," Trina inquired, "Have you ever been to Paris?"

"No, I have not had the pleasure." He took a sip of his soup and wiped his mouth with his napkin. "Miss O'Connor, have you read *The Thirty-nine Steps*?"

Allison looked up wide-eyed, apparently appalled by his contrived harassment. "Unlike my mother, I have *no* interest in murder mysteries. Now, if you do not mind, I was under the impression that the soup was to be eaten while it was still hot." She continued to sip it.

The other three diners were amazed that the schoolmaster appeared to be unaffected by Allison's curt responses.

"I found the novel to be quite the opposite and very enlightening," Joel commented.

Naomi, Edward, and Trina held their spoon's in midair. Dare he disturb her again?

He did.

"Exactly what prose do you find to be worthwhile?"

Allison placed her spoon beside her bowl and slowly addressed her mother.

"Mother, would you please ask that the second course be served?"

Edward quickly interrupted, "Allison, Joel asked you a question."

"Yes, I believe that we are all aware of that fact—but I, for one, do not enjoy being grilled while I am dining." Allison turned to Joel and glared. "You do understand?"

Joel smiled. "Of course, my mistake. I shall wait until you are finished."

Edward broke into laughter; Naomi snickered behind her napkin.

Trina stared inquisitively at her friend, dumbfounded by her uncommon behavior, and then blurted out with enthusiasm, "I just finished reading D. H. Lawrence's *The Rainbow!*"

Joel, still smiling at the obstinate Miss O'Connor, made no acknowledgement of Miss Dunmore's admission.

After a brief discussion of stamp collecting, and the stolen Irish Crown jewels, Allison finally returned to the conversation.

"We all seemed to be finished with our meal, might we have the afters served?"

Jules was summoned and the tea and raspberry scones were delivered on a silver tray.

Joel took another shot at lighting a fire under Allison.

"I could not help but notice that you attended the McDonnally wedding...*unaccompanied.*"

Allison's face took on one of a raging, mad dog.

"The details of *my* social life are none of your business! Now, if you will excuse me." She slid her chair back and marched from the room.

"I will be calling on you, later!" Joel called after her. He turned back to the shocked faces in triplicate. "The meal was delightful—as was the company. Charming girl," he said with remarkable sincerity.

That evening in the drawing room, Naomi hummed a lullaby while knitting a sleeve of a tiny pale yellow sweater.

"Persistent fellow, that Joel," Edward commented behind the cover of *The Camp Magazine.*

"Yes, he is that, but I am not certain that our daughter is appreciative of his apparent intentions. I have never known her to be so outwardly rude. I was so embarrassed. I will have to apologize for her, tomorrow."

"You need not bother—her rudeness seems to fuel his persistence. He seemed to enjoy her callous behavior. A glutton for punishment, I believe. Strange bloke, that man."

"Much more clever and outspoken, than I ever imagined. I told Trina that he was a shy sort. She shall never believe another word out of my mouth." She shook her head and dropped a stitch. "Oops." She quickly recovered it and purled the next row.

She rested her knitting on her blossoming belly and asked, "Darling, why would a man tolerate such insolence from a woman?"

He cleared his throat and remained hidden behind the novel.

"Edward Caleb, I am *not* that intolerable."

He peeked over the top edge. "Nay dear, you are not. In answer to your question, I think that it is the challenge. Remember Hiram and Abigail's courtship?"

"Dear, I think it inappropriate to mention Hiram's past affairs, so soon after his wedding," she reprimanded him. "After all, have you forgotten how that relationship ended?"

He lowered the book. "To Joel's dismay this one may end before it begins. All the same, I believe that Allison is baiting the trap—playing 'hard-to-get.'"

"You must be joking. Our daughter has no interest whatsoever in the man."

"Why do you believe this?"

"Because she told me so. Allison never plays games. She is straightforward. I know her, but for the life of me, I do not know why she harbors any animosity for him. She has not known him long enough to form an opinion."

"Dearest, after tonight, I am certain that she has."

The next evening, Trina and Allison ordered a carriage to take them to the inn, as they had planned the night before. Trina had used the excuse to engage in a conversation about their earlier trip to America, as a reason for the outing. The carriage rattled along the cobblestones.

"Trina, I cannot tell you how grand it is to have someone my own age with which to converse, again. I no sooner left you in America and I was back to this vacuum of boredom."

"It *is* good to be back... You shall never guess who I met at the mercantile."

"Someone of interest in *Lochmoor Glen*? I cannot imagine."

"Henry McTavish."

"I am surprised. He has kept to himself recently. How is he? Upset about he and Mercy?"

"No...he was preparing to run an errand for Mr. Dugan. I think that he will be gone for quite a while."

"He is probably sick of seeing Mercy and Guillaume traipsing about."

"Guillaume and Mercy?"

"Yes, they are combining forces: McDonnally and Stockdale—quite the monetary match."

"How are *you* dealing with the match, Allison?"

"I have no opinion about Mr. Zigmann and his affairs."

"You certainly have an opinion about Joel Merriman."

"I would think that you would, too, considering his despicable behavior in my home."

"I have none. However, I do plan to meet with him this week."

"For what purpose?" Allison asked indignantly.

"Oh, I thought that I might offer my assistance with a dance and music class for the children."

Allison turned to the window. "Are you going

to see Tavy when he returns?"

"He alluded to it."

"You should. He positively adored you at one time. Mercy is no longer of interest to him." She turned back. "I thought we were to discuss the trip to America? Did you discover why you were asked to make the trip?"

"Kin...that is all."

"Do not speak of it so trivially. I wish that I knew my relatives. Being orphaned, you never know. I may pass my kin on the street and be none the wiser."

"You are a blessed McDonnally, now, Allison. That is more than enough family anyone would need."

The carriage stopped at the inn and the coachmen opened the door and helped them down. Inside, their conversation continued over a cup of tea.

"Allison, someday, once you marry and have your own family, I believe that void of being orphaned will diminish."

Allison remained solemn.

"Why were you so dreadful to Joel?" Trina inquired.

"Joel, again? Did you not see how horribly obnoxious the lad was?"

"Lad? Are you going blind, as well? He is a fine figure of a man."

"Man? Phew! I would guess he is only—"

"Much younger than Hiram or George Hicks?"

"We are not discussing my past. Besides, age is irrelevant. He is a common schoolmaster, Trina."

Trina straightened in her chair and knitted

her brows. "First of all, Joel is older than either of us and secondly, were you not the one advising me to seek out Henry, a *common* sailor?" she raised her voice. "I am beginning to understand. You have lost not one McDonnally man, but two, with Guillaume out of your life, and now you will settle for nothing less."

"I have heard enough of your analyzing. I am going home. Are you coming?"

They each paid for their own bill and went directly to the awaiting carriage without speaking.

Chapter VI

"Uphill Battle"

"Mid groves of green that fringe its side,
Dark sails that gleam on
Oceans heaving breast
From the glad fisher-barks
that homeward glide
To make Clovelly shores at
pleasant Evening-tide."

—Robert Stephen Hawker

When they returned to Brachney Hall, Trina followed Allison up the staircase.

"Allison you received a great gift in being adopted into the McDonnally clan. No matter who you marry, you will never want for anything. Why not set your sights on having it all, having that special someone to love you—someone you truly love in return, despite his station in life."

Allison turned to her when Trina reached the landing. Allison made no reply.

"Allison,perhaps, Joel is not the man for you. I am not suggesting that you lower your standards, just do not make that standard a monetary one," Trina said gently.

"Do not trouble yourself with my social life."

"I am only making an observation."

"Why not observe Tavy instead of me—he is free now," Allison said pointedly. "Or is a poor sailor not good enough?" she added sharply and started to walk away.

"Considering our past, Henry may or may not be the one for me, but the schoolmaster maybe worth pursuing," Trina said casually.

Allison turned abruptly with a look of outrage and shouted, "Stay away from him, Trina! He is...he is a lunatic! He is daft!" She ran on toward her bedchamber and slammed the door behind her.

Naomi cracked open her bedroom door. "What has happened?" She yawned.

"I am sorry we wakened you, but your daughter has just had an epiphany."

"What?"

"Allison despises Joel, but oddly does not want anyone else to pursue him. Good night, Mrs.

McDonnally."

Naomi looked toward Allison's bedchamber. "Hmm? Good night, Trina."

Trina entered her room and closed the door. She walked over and sat on the edge of the bed. Henry McTavish was as handsome as ever, but he was definitely opinionated about mixing the social classes. This was a problem. Guillaume, her first love, was no longer available, either. Not that she was seeking a husband or even a beau, but she had considered a life with both of them. Henry, the sincere sailor, would no longer be a candidate—not since her discovery in America.

She squatted down beside the bed, leaned over and removed the suitcase. She heaved it upon the quilt, opened the latches, and slowly opened the lid, wishing the contents had miraculously disappeared—but it had not. The stacks of hundreds of thousands of bills lay before her. *Thank you Lord Dunmore—but no thank you.*

Sole heir to the Dunmore estate, Trina was a very wealthy woman. She had never wanted for anything; her immediate family had left her a sufficient fortune, however, by no means comparable to the millions that lay before her. She had guarded it with her life on the return trip to Scotland, but regretted its presence. Money had destroyed her great uncle's life and she feared that it would hers, as well. Lord Dunmore was banished from Scotland for his wrongdoings, leaving behind this fortune of questionable origin. The lawyers assured her that it was legally hers. *Legally*, according to those in the United States, but what about to those of Scotland Yard?

She had been advised to take her inheritance

in the form of a note, but there was something highly irregular and suspicious about the law firm, so she took it in cash. She had left America immediately after being awarded the sum and booked passage on two different ships: one first-class, and one third-class. At the last minute, she stepped aboard the latter to protect her interest.

Lord Dunmore, I think that you may have done more than I care to know, she thought, closing the latches.

This problem was overwhelming, to say the least, but Allison's was manageable. That night, Trina Dunmore became Allison's self-appointed conscience. She was determined to make her friend come to grips with her actual attraction for the outspoken schoolmaster.

How was she to do this? She devised a simple plan, but there was a nagging sense that it could backfire. After all, Trina was not a homely sort and had quite a lot to offer. The very worst that could happen was that Joel Merriman may make an about face and *she,* instead of Allison would become the source of his affections. However, this could easily be resolved, if necessary. Her plan would commence first thing in the morning.

The next day, immediately after breakfast, she ordered a carriage to McDonnally Manor, directly outside the dining room door—so that Allison would be aware of her destination. Trina was confident that the first step in her plot had gone off without a hitch. She waved to a scowling Allison, postured at the sidelight of the portal.

Once Trina entered the McDonnally west

wing, where the school was located, she spoke to Livia about her interest in volunteering to help with the music class including voice, dance, and piano. During such a time of teacher shortages, Livia naturally welcomed her charitable offer and was certain that Joel would agree.

"I will tell him that you wish to speak with him. Go on ahead and wait in the conservatory."

"Thank you, Livia."

Joel arrived before she had a chance to sit down.

"Mr. Merriman."

"Joel, please. Now, what is that you care to discuss, Miss Dunmore?"

"Joel, I could not help noticing that you and my friend, Allison, were, shall I say, at odds with one another at Brachney Hall."

"Miss Dunmore, I cannot understand it, myself. She seems to...to detest me. I suppose I was a little pushy. I never meant to go that far with it. I could not help myself. Lighting a fire under Miss O'Connor produces a beautiful flame. She is such a gorgeous spitfire." The vigor in his voice faded. "I have probably destroyed any chance of a future with her," he added solemnly.

"Oh, I can assure you that is *not* the case."

"No?"

"Absolutely not. Why only last night, we were discussing her feelings for you. I believe that she is quite taken with you."

"*Indeed.* Exactly, what did she say?" he asked eagerly.

"As her friend and confidant, you understand that I cannot reveal the details."

"Naturally." He paced in a small circle and

stopped, steepling his fingers. "Miss Dunmore, you have made the perfect day for me. I have searched my soul for a reason as to why she did not approve of me. I thought all hope was lost."

Searched his soul?

He stood in deep thought, peering out the window with his arms folded across his chest.

"What are you going to do with this new information?" she asked coyly.

"Miss Dunmore, as a friend and now confidant, you surely cannot expect me to reveal the details," he said, wearing a Cheshire grin.

"Naturally." Trina smiled, though she was disappointed in his discretion.

"It has been lovely, Miss Dunmore. Now, if you will please excuse me—I need to—I have to be going!" he said with the anxiety of a horse chomping at the bit.

"Have a wonderful afternoon!"

"Most definitely!" he called, running from the west wing. "Please, tell Livia, that I shall return, later!"

She turned to catch a glimpse of the fleeing schoolmaster racing down the corridor and returned to the schoolroom where Livia met her.

"Was he pleased?"

"Oh, yes, he was definitely pleased," Trina replied with an air of mystery. "He has left the school for a while." She smiled victoriously. "Livia, yours may not be the only wedding this year."

Livia's eyes widened. "Oh, my," is all she dared say.

Once again, a comment such as Trina's could not remain latent in Lochmoor Glen. By sunset, word had traveled from Livia to Eloise, to Harriet Dugan to all of Lochmoor Glen and beyond. However, before the residents of Brachney Hall got word, Allison and her mother shared a heart-to-heart conversation in Naomi's boudoir.

"Mother?"

"Yes, darling."

"How are you feeling to day?"

"Fine. Why do you ask? Do I not look well?"

"No, no. You look the picture of health. Quite beautiful, as always. I was only curious...you being with child."

Naomi took Allison's hand and walked her over to the couch where they sat. "Curious about how it feels?"

Allison nodded.

"Of course before there are a great deal of noticeable physical changes with which to deal. But there is also a great sense of mystery. It is difficult to describe. I am not the same. Initially, there was this incredible joy—this inability to stop smiling. It was as if I had a special secret, although it was common knowledge. There is this tiny person who I am carrying who I do not know, but love so very much. Now, that I feel the baby move," she said, placing her hands on her belly, "and see that he or she is growing, I feel even more connected and like a special protector of this helpless little stranger. Am I making sense?"

Allison smiled and nodded, again.

"Baby, the anticipation is unbelievable. It is like a gift that you know is the best present that you will ever receive, yet you must carry it around for—well, as though you are given a Christmas gift and have to wait until nearly the following year to open it. Sometimes, you forget about it, being involved in routine activities, but sure enough, a reminder springs up: ill-fitting clothes, seeing another with child, or an infant or perhaps a sudden pain."

"Are you anxious for it to be over?"

"Yes, part of me is so incredibly impatient—wanting to see and hold this bairn. On the other hand, I fear that I shall miss this feeling of having my baby tucked safe inside and feeling so blessed."

Allison remained solemn.

"What is wrong, my dear?"

"I was only thinking...I wonder if my mother felt that way," she said somberly.

"Oh, darling, I am certain of it." She took Allison's hand in hers. "You may not have had your mother very long in this world, but you had a wonderful nine month bond with her."

Her eyes welled up. "You and I did not share that bond."

Naomi put her arm around Allison's shoulders and explained, trying to withhold her tears. "No, that is true, but I believe that bond that you shared with your mother and the one I shared with mine, your grandmother Beatrice, prepared us for our relationship. The good Lord planned for our meeting. We were drawn together as mother and daughter—you had lost your mother, as I had temporarily lost mine. It was all very natural. We had experienced the internal bond, but the present was opened just a few years later. She smiled and wiped a tear from her daughter's cheek. Does that make sense?"

"Yes, Mama."

***

The night before the trip to Clovelly, Rufus tossed and turned in anticipation of the upcoming adventure. Several times, he rushed Tavy's bed with a slew of questions regarding the journey. This would be the first time that the little boy had stepped off the soil of Lochmoor Glen. He finally drifted off with visions of unusual looking Clovelly residents, animals, and surroundings. It would only be a few hours before he discovered that the little village of Clovelly was truly, remarkably special in its own right.

Tavy and his little red-haired companion entered the cobblestone streets of Clovelly, on foot.

"I ne'er seen such a place. Why would they build it on this bloody hill?" Rufus asked.

"Ye need not say 'bloody.' It doesna sound good from a lad's mouth. I would catch it from Ma, if she heard it."

"But why?"

"Because I said so."

"Nay, why is it on a hill?"

"The hill was here, as was the ocean and I suspect that the only place to build was up."

Rufus eyed a donkey towing a sledge of packages.

"Ye see, Rufus, it is so steep that they canna use carts with wheels."

"Is that our donkey?"

"Nay, he is yonder, in the livery." Tavy pointed to a sign on the right.

Rufus ran ahead without much effort. Tavy shook his head and trudged on. When Rufus reached the livery, three lads noted the newcomer with scrutiny.

"Who might you be?" one Clovelly boy asked Rufus.

"Me name is Rufus of Lochmoor Glen."

"Lochmoor Glen? Is that the residence of the McDonnallys?" the shortest of the three asked his companion.

"Yes."

The older turned to Rufus. "Are you acquainted with Master McDonnally?"

"Which one?" Rufus asked.

"Master Hiram McDonnally, of course?"

"Aye, 'tis a good friend o' mine," Rufus quickly responded, his fingers crossed behind him.

The boys looked at one another, dubious of his response. Rufus smiled in satisfaction.

"What is your business in Clovelly?" the youngest asked.

"We are fetchin' a donkey."

Tavy came up from behind him.

"Is that man your father?" the oldest asked.

Rufus paused and shook his head. "A mate o' mine."

"I'll be inside," Tavy interrupted, patting Rufus's shoulder and then entering the livery.

"Where is your father?" The middle-sized boy asked.

"Me pa is in heaven."

"Does your mother know that you ran away to Clovelly with *that* man?" the older boy asked.

"Nay...maybe—she is in heaven, too."

The middle-sized boy snickered, "So you are an orphan—a beggar of the streets."

Rufus's face reddened, "Nay! I'm not!"

"Yes, you are," the younger chimed in.

"Come along," the eldest boy ordered the other two. "We shan't associate with the likes of him. Our parents would not approve—bad influence." They all laughed and ran down the hill.

Rufus stood speechless, a pain in his stomach, as though the passing donkey had kicked him. He felt a hand ruffling his hair and looked up to see Tavy standing over him.

"Mate, look at this."

Still red-faced, Rufus wiped his eyes.

Tavy bent down. "Carrot Top, what has happened?"

Rufus clutched Tavy's neck like a lifeline and sobbed. Tavy held him close. "There, there, laddie. N' more o' that. Donkeys dunna like cryin'. Ye had better stop."

Rufus pulled himself together and peeked over Tavy's shoulder at the four-legged beast. He reached out cautiously to touch the velvet muzzle. The large brown eyes stared at him with seemingly knowing sympathy. The long-eared creature gently licked Rufus's hand, wet with salty tears and then began to nibble at his finger.

"Hey!" Rufus withdrew his hand.

Tavy laughed, "The good Lord didna give donkeys hands, but he gave them mouths and they make good use o' them to get into mischief."

Rufus kept a close eye on that clever mouth.

"He may be a mischief maker, not unlike yourself," Tavy teased, "but he can become yer best friend."

Rufus reached up and slid his hand across the vertical mane. "Will his mane lie down like Hunter's, someday?"

"Nay, a bit like yers, it stands straight up."

Tavy winked at him. "We had better make haste, we hae a long journey ahead o' us."

The trio moved slowly down the hill. Rufus paused when he spotted the rude peers across the street.

"Orphan!" the youngest called.

Now realizing the source of Rufus's early outburst, Tavy glared at the three.

"Ye talking to me?" Tavy called back. He then pulled his rucksack from his back. The three scallywags cowered in fear. Tavy pulled out a long thin box. He held it, slapping it against his palm, staring at the boys. They darted into the bakery behind them. Their heads slowly rose above the windowsill to view the furious man from Lochmoor Glen. Tavy handed the box to Rufus who regarded it curiously.

Tavy smiled, "'Tis for you, fellow orphan."

Rufus's face lit up. He quickly removed the lid. Tavy turned slowly, glowered at the insolent lads, and watched their heads raise and their jaws drop when Rufus removed the handsome brass and wood spyglass.

"'Tis the fancy one from the mercantile!" Rufus exclaimed.

"Aye, the verra one."

Rufus hugged Tavy's waist. "Thank ye!"

Rufus handed the box and the lead rope to Tavy. He lifted the glass to his eye, turned to admire the envious audience posted in the bakery window, and grinned with pure satisfaction.

On route to Lochmoor Glen, Tavy's wagon, with the little donkey riding in the makeshift travel stall, stopped in Eyemouth to check out the schooner "gift." As suspected, the bow was rotten, the mainsail broken, along with other assorted defects from years on the seas.

They continued on the journey homeward. Joseph was the first to greet the weary travelers with the prize donkey from Clovelly. He was pleased as punch, but the receiver of the gray and brown bristly-haired, Christmas present, was not.

"Joseph Dugan, yer not pullin' the wool o'er me eyes. Ye didna want that creature for me—ye wanted more mules," she scorned.

"Aye, so I did and 'tis not such a dreadful idea. Ye need anot'er mule to pull ye to the village mercantile, while Jock is workin' wi' me in the fields."

Rufus sat at the kitchen table withholding comment, but felt a number of remarks bubbling up—ready to fly through his lips. If he was to be a part of this family, he would have to exercise restraint, no matter how silly Ma "Dukan" behaved.

She narrowed her eyes at the donkey grazing in the yard.

"Does it ever stop movin'?" she grumbled.

"Nay," Joseph replied.

She returned to her stove and removed a pan of hot scones from the oven. She threw a disapproving glance at her husband and barked, "If you wouldna hae sent this lad on a wild goose-chase to Clovelly, he wouldna hae lost his chance wi' Trina!"

"'Twas not a wild goose chase, 'twas a donkey—" Rufus began.

Tavy cut him off with a quick hand placed over his mouth. "Ma, what d' ye mean 'chance wi'

Trina?'"

"While ye were gone donkey fetchin', Trina accepted anot'r proposal."

"Proposal? What's that?" Rufus intervened.

"Married? To whom?" Tavy demanded.

"The schoolmaster—Merriman."

"Merriman?" Tavy could not believe it. Trina had been back for such a short time. "Excuse me; I need to water the donkey."

"He can drink from the horse trough," Joseph insisted.

"Nay, the livery man said donkeys willna drink dirty water," Rufus explained.

"What?" Harriet spun around.

Joseph gave Rufus a nudge, "Ye need to be helpin' Tavy. Out wi' ye!"

Rufus snatched a scone and ran outside. He walked up behind Tavy.

"Did ye love, Miss Dunmore?" he asked timidly.

"Nay, Carrot Top. I am concerned for her. She's barely acquainted wi' the bloke."

"Is he a bloke?"

"Nay... ye need not worry 'bout it."

"Rufus!" Harriet called from the backdoor. "Come here!"

"Aye. Mum!" he ran to her.

"I want ye to deliver this basket o' scones to the Wheaton farm for me. Ye may eat one—only one more. Now be off wi' ye."

Rufus ran to the barn and tugged on Tavy's sleeve. "Can I take the donkey along?"

"Why? Do ye want to show it off?"

"Aye," he said shyly, "To show Jeanie."

Tavy untied the lead rope and handed it to

Rufus.

"Come along, Pete," Rufus coaxed.

"Pete?"

"He would be needin' a name, since he's a orphan," Rufus explained.

"Aye, he would. 'Pete'—'tis done. Get along ye two."

The relatively short walk to the Wheaton farm, took longer than Rufus expected. He learned the valuable lesson: why donkeys are said to be stubborn. When Rufus wasn't trying to tug Pete away from the patches of grass along the side of the road, he was struggling to keep the donkey's head out of the basket of scones. He was now two scones short, as Pete was not satisfied with the one he shared with Rufus.

The Wheaton cottage was a welcoming sight where Maryanne and Allison greeted him from the porch swing. Rufus proudly led the donkey.

"Hello, Rufus!"

"Hello, Miss Connor, Miss Wheaton!"

"What do ye hae there?" Maryanne called, leaving the swing.

"Ma Dukan's Christmas donkey. These scones are for ye." He handed her the basket. "Where's Jeanie?"

"Sorry, she has gone to the mercantile wi' her Pa and one o' her ducks. Shirley, I believe," Maryanne giggled.

Rufus kicked the dirt and tightened his lips with disappointment.

Allison walked down the steps. "Where did she get the donkey?"

"Me and Tavy fetched him."

"He is adorable. What's his name?"

"Pete. He's an orphan like me and Tavy."

Allison studied the boy's face, thinking, *so am I.*

"Where did Tavy find him?" Maryanne asked.

"All the way in Clovelly, where the street is on a big hill."

"Did you have a good time?" Allison asked.

"I did. Tavy gave me the spyglass from the mercantile. But now Tavy is a bit down in the mouth."

"Why?" the women inquired in unison.

"Mr. Merriman stole Trina from him while we were in Clovelly."

"Tri—Trina?" Allison stuttered.

"Aye, they are gettin' married."

"Who is?" Allison demanded a little louder than she intended.

"Trina and Mr. Merriman."

Allison's heart sank. She was speechless.

Rufus watched her run finger along the cross on the donkey's back and commented, "Tavy says he has Jesus' cross because he wanted to help Jesus carry the cross, but they wouldna let him. The donkey was sad, but stayed wi' Jesus, and the cross shadow fell on his back and ne'r left, forever and ever."

"That is a wonderful story, Rufus," Maryanne said, leading Rufus away, concerned for Allison and her obvious distress about the news regarding Trina and Joel. "Please thank Mrs. Dugan for the scones."

"I will. Tell 'em g'day, Pete."

To the women's surprise, Pete let out a braying farewell while Tavy waved.

***

The following afternoon on her departure from the music class at the school, Trina crossed paths with Hiram, returning from his rounds on the farms.

"Congrats, Miss Dunmore! I heard the grand news. No one is happier than I...uh, you have chosen a good man—Merriman!" He continued down the hall, smiling and delighted that Livia's admirer would soon have a wife of his own.

Trina was bowled over by the comment. Eloise, feather dusting, distracted her before she had a chance to think it through.

"Miss Dunmore, how long has this been going on?" She giggled and then drew a remorseful expression. "I am sorry, 'tis none of my business." She hurried off to the study to continue her chores.

Trina squinted, completely baffled by Eloise's remark. She trailed the housekeeper into the study.

"Mrs. Zigmann, how long has what been going on?"

Eloise swallowed and replied, "You and Mr. Merriman."

"Joel and I?"

"The master's wife mentioned, in passing, that you two are to be wed this year."

Trina closed her eyes and then began to laugh. When she finally caught her breath, it dawned on her. If Eloise believed this, her best friend Harriet did, too. This meant Tavy and possibly Allison had heard the same misconstrued rumor. No gossip was sacred in Lochmoor Glen.

"Oh, no! I have to go!"

When Trina arrived at Brachney Hall, she was having second thoughts about squelching the rumor; a little jealousy may inspire Allison to reveal her true colors—her honest feelings for Joel. This may speed things up in her plan to get the couple together and relieve Tavy from any suspicions that she and Joel were involved. She entered the parlor and lay in wait for Allison's response. It did not take long.

Allison appeared in the hall doorway.

Chapter VII

"Through the Grapevine"

"If just one ship I have at sea
Should come a-sailing home to me,
Ah, well! The storm clouds then might frown
For if the others all went down
Still rich and proud and glad I'd be,
If that one ship came back to me."

—Ella Wheeler Wilcox

"Trina Dunmore, I need to speak with you," Allison commanded.

Trina remained sitting, unscathed.

"Yes, Allison," she said calmly.

"Are you insane?" Allison charged.

"Whatever do you mean?"

"Marrying Joel? You barely know the man."

"I have been working with him at the school. I thought that you knew."

"You cannot do this—it is all wrong!" She marched to the window and back. "As your friend, I must insist and advise you to end this relationship immediately!"

"But Allison—"

"You are much too young to marry, Trina."

"Sophia is younger than either of us and she is the mother of three children."

"That was a highly irregular situation—having triplets. Trina, trust me, he is not right for you."

"*Who* is he right for, in your fine opinion?"

"That I do not know, but certainly not *you*."

"And why is that?"

"It is obvious. You are a well-travelled woman of the world. You need someone of a higher station or you shall be miserable. Not a lowly schoolmaster."

"You had suggested Henry, earlier."

"I...I changed my mind. He is not acceptable, either."

"I think that I could adapt. Joel is very sweet."

"Sweetness will not provide you with the comforts already to which you are accustomed."

"I have all the comforts and he is so handsome and charming."

"Yes, he is, but you cannot base a relationship

on mere attraction."

"Allison, I am not a hypocrite. As I said before, there are more important factors in a marriage than equivalent social status and wealth."

"Yes, but think about it. Could you be truly happy?"

"If the relationship is based on love, the rest is secondary."

Allison stared inquisitively, then asked hesitantly, "Do you really believe that, Trina?"

Trina instantly noted Allison's loss of conviction in her tone.

"Yes. The attraction and the sweetness feeds the love. The love lessens and supersedes the need for material things. All you need is each other and respect for one another. Joel has an honorable position in the community and he is far from destitute. He offers an adequate income."

Allison sat down in the rocking chair and began to rock. She quickly fell into deep thought, mulling over Trina's philosophy. Trina watched and waited.

Finally, Allison stopped rocking and turned to Trina.

"Do you think it possible?" Allison asked timidly.

"Yes, I think that you and Joel were made for each other. I have never witnessed a better choreographed debate session than yours and his, here, the other night," she laughed.

"Joel and I? Who said anything about me and Joel?"

"Your expression speaks for itself."

"Do you really, truly believe it would work out, between us?"

"Yes, and there is no basis in that silly rumor about Joel and I. We are barely friends."

"But he probably despises me, after his visit here."

"No, on the contrary, he wants you, as much as ever. He confessed this to me."

Just then, they noticed Jules hovering outside the room, trying not to interrupt, but anxious about an envelope that he was holding.

"Come in, Jules," Allison spoke up.

"I have a letter for you, Miss Dunmore."

Trina left Allison to contemplate her future with Joel, and read the post in the privacy of her bedchamber. She sat on the bed and removed the seal from the envelope. Her heart sped, reading the ominous threats. She ran to her bureau, snatched her pocketbook, and stuffed the letter inside.

"Henry, I have to see you," she muttered aloud to the empty room.

Tavy had dealt with all phases of treachery. Hopefully, he could advise her.

Trina bid the catatonic Allison farewell and ordered the coachman to drop her at the gate of the Dugan cottage. She prayed that Tavy would be there. She rushed to the door and knocked. Harriet answered.

"Miss Dunmore?" she said with suspicion.

"Hello. Is Henry here?"

"Aye, he is out back. He—"

Trina was off. Harriet moved quickly through the house to the kitchen window to observe the confrontation.

"Henry!"

Tavy looked up from grooming Jock. He could

not bring himself to greet her.

"Henry, I need your help!"

"I shan't be the best man! I dunna care if he has n' kin or friends here."

She took hold of his arm.

"Henry, Joel and I are not engaged. It is nothing but a rumor. I assure you that Joel is interested in Allison and her in him." She took a deep breath. "I am in grave need of your help."

His scowl faded. "Come into the barn." He offered her a seat on a nail keg.

"Thank you. Henry, I am in a terrible mess. When I went to America—I was awarded an inheritance."

He glanced to the roof. "Aye, a terrible thing, bein' rich," he said snidely.

"Henry, this is a serious situation! I have money, more than you can imagine! It is under my bed at Brachney Hall and before I came to see you, I received a threatening letter! They are coming for the money! They say that it is rightfully theirs."

"Who?"

"I do not know. They gave no evidence to their identity."

"If it is legally yers—"

"I am not sure. My great uncle left it to me. He was somewhat of a pirate and banished from the British Isles. I have no proof that he came by it honestly." She took his hand, "Henry, I do not want it!"

"Then give it to 'em."

"What? How do we know that it is rightfully theirs?"

"Then contact Scotland Yard."

"Yes, they will investigate it, but what do I do

with the money in the mean time? I dare not take it with me. I am certainly being watched. I cannot leave it at Brachney Hall and endanger the McDonnallys."

"Ye women and yer bags o' money," he protested, remembering the episode with Mercy. "If yer bein' watched, they need to see ye move it from Brachney Hall."

They turned suddenly to a rustling in the loft. Rufus's smiling, freckled face appeared. Trina and Tavy exchanged a mutual look of concern. Their little mischievous friend was now privy to the dire situation and vital information.

"Rufus, come down here," Tavy commanded.

The fearless lad leaped from the loft, nearly causing heart failure to his audience below.

"How much did ye hear?" Tavy inquired.

"Ne'er missed a word!" he announced proudly, obviously intrigued by the drama.

After dubiously swearing Rufus to secrecy, the couple sent him out to walk Pete while they contrived a plan to report to Scotland Yard.

With Trina's permission, Tavy met with Edward to explain the grim situation. Anxious to protect his home and family, Edward agreed to assist. Word was that two strangers were staying at the inn and offering no information about their agenda. More than likely they were responsible for the threats.

As scheduled, Edward, Trina, and Tavy met at Brachney Hall. The three staged an argument in the drive in front of the mansion. In reality they were discussing the details of their plan with hopes that the two culprits were observing from the most likely location—the woods between the estate and Hiram's. Jules exited the mansion, looked both directions, and then rushed two carpetbags to the parked carriage. Naomi followed. Edward removed his Panama hat, kissed his wife goodbye, and climbed inside with Tavy; Angus rode above with the coachmen. Everyone was certain that the two highwaymen would not attempt to accost Master Edward McDonnally. The booty would not be worth the repercussions.

The trip to Eyemouth went without incidence. The rest was history in the making.

Trina was relieved to see Tavy and Edward arrive home safely from the mission. Edward left Tavy and Trina to their welcoming embrace and hurried off to see his expecting wife.

"Henry, I am anxious to hear every detail. Come sit with me," Trina implored.

They walked through the side yard.

"Where's Rufus?" Tavy asked.

"I left them a half hour ago. He and Eloise were battling over the preparation of sweets. Rufus preferred uncooked dough to the baked goods."

"As did I, as a lad."

They sat down on the bench overlooking the pond.

"So did they try to stop you en route to Eyemouth? Did you ever get a glimpse of them?"

"Trina, please, I promise to give ye all the details."

"Sorry, go on."

"Aye they were watchin', but they didna attempt to detain us. When we arrived, the coachmen drove directly to the sheriff's office, where the two carpetbags were placed in his care, for safe keepin'. We went on to the inn to eat. Edward checked in to rest and I visited wi' Aaron O'Grady."

"Who is Aaron O'Grady?"

"Shipbuilder and repairman. I also filled his head with false information. Told him that two blokes were seekin' me out for a debt, they were tryin' to collect and I needed the *Kinney May, the* schooner that Dobby left me, repaired. I took him down to the dock to see it. After a brief exam, he said it was beyond repair. O' course, this is what I expected."

"So the two men witnessed all of this and he would tell them, when they made the inquiry, that you were planning to use it to escape from them with the money, despite the boat's condition."

"*Ship.* Exactly. The weather was made to order. A storm blew in, that evenin'."

"But, hold on! He did not repair the schooner?"

"Nay, 'twas too damaged."

"But you could have been killed!"

"I'm here and verra much alive."

"What about the boat? Did they see you?"

"*Ship.* Aye, they saw me load the bags on board. They followed me, at a distance from the sheriff's office to the dock. I was untyin' the *Kinney May* and launched out to sea before they blinked an eye. The wind was portside and leeward."

"From which direction was that?"

"Comin' from the west. It took us out to sea before—"

"Us?"

"Me and the *Kinney May.*"

"Oh."

"As planned, she was only afloat for a few minutes at about nine knots before she capsized. The carpetbags, weighted with sand, sank like rocks. The waves carried her a good distance. Bein' night, stormy, and no moon, only a few lightnin' strikes hinted at me whereabouts."

She jumped to her feet. "You were out swimming in that *cold* water with lightning striking all about you?"

"Calm yourself. I swam safely, unnoticed to shore. They thought I went down wi' me ship. Now, sit back down."

She did, harboring great feelings of guilt for having put him in such grave danger.

"Next mornin', they were draggin' a net for the bags, I'm guessin'. While the one was steerin' a dory, the other was swimmin' all over creation searchin' for the bags. 'Twas quite a sight to see."

"And Edward?"

"He had left for home, after visitin' the coroner's office to report me death. I am legally off to meet me maker in that big sea in the sky," he laughed.

"That is not amusing, Henry," she said somberly.

He put his arm around her and gave her a squeeze. "And I caught up wi' Edward later and we returned."

"On foot?"

"No, love. I bought a horse from a farmer a couple of miles outside o' town."

"What if he had refused to sell you one?" she panicked.

"But he did. Now, I must fetch Rufus. I hope

he didna feel that I abandoned him."

"No, he was kept busy. Naomi put him to work, painting a mural for the nursery wall. Come, you have to see it. You are now immortal."

"Me?"

"Yes, you adorn the nursery wall, bigger—much bigger than life," she giggled.

Trina took his arm and they walked up to the rear entrance of the house.

"I didna forget him. I bought him a travel present."

"Travel present?"

"Aye, a gift from me travels."

"What is it, if I may ask?"

"A shark tooth necklace."

"Impressive. What about me?" she teased.

To her surprise, he stopped and reached into the front pocket of his jacket. "These."

"Henry, I was not serious," she said, embarrassed.

He handed her a palm-sized bundle tied in brown paper. She carefully opened it. With wide-eyed wonder, she lifted them from the paper.

"Henry, they are positively gorgeous!"

She quickly pulled her hair back on the sides with the pair of two metal combs adorned with abalone shell pieces.

"Verra bonnie. You look like a mermaid from the sea."

"Truly?" she asked coyly.

"Aye, ye do."

She stood on tiptoe and kissed his cheek. "Thank you, Henry—for these and for your courageous help." He only smiled.

"Let's see me handsome portrait, then fetch

the artist. I shan't hae much time wi' him before we need to leave for Scotland Yard."

She smiled and nodded.

Tavy was pleased with his creative image, but wondered if Rufus really remembered him being *that* large. Tavy relieved Eloise of her little assistant who proudly donned his new necklace and sang with Tavy all the way home:

> *"The big ship sails,*
> *Through the alley, alley oh*
> *The alley, alley oh*
> *The alley, alley oh*
>
> *The big ship sails*
> *Through the alley, alley oh*
> *On the last day of September.*
>
> *The captain says,*
> *"It will never, never do,*
> *Never, never, do*
> *Never, never, do*
>
> *The captain says,*
> *"It will never, never do,*
> *On the last day of September.*
>
> *The big ship sank*
> *To the bottom of the sea*
> *The bottom of the sea*
> *The bottom of the sea*
>
> *The big ship sank*
> *To the bottom of the sea*
> *On the last day of September."*

***

At the Sierzik home, Sophia's afternoon lullabies had lost their "lulling power." The advanced crawling stage had crept up all too quickly. The idea of sitting still in a rocker was almost obsolete. Zanya and Ruthia were now moving freely about. However, Von was a bit of a late bloomer—which did little to boost his father's ego. Von would remain seated in the middle of the floor, engrossed in examination of whatever toy was available. Ruthia found her brother's slow development to be to her advantage. She was often caught watching him and studying the toy in his possession. Seconds later, she would snatch the toy without warning and creep off with it, giggling over her victory. To his father's dismay, his son demonstrated no honor to the name "Manstrong." Von was reduced to tears, sulking. On witnessing this ritual, Rahzvon often picked up another toy for his son and explained that he needed to fight for his rights. Naturally, this advice fell on deaf ears.

His mother's only comment was, "I do not know where he gets this behavior. It is definitely not on the McDonnally side. We do not let anyone walk on us," she added casually.

"I know," Rahzvon muttered.

One particular day, after one of Ruthia's power struggles with her brother over a coveted toy, Rahzvon lifted his son to the window to distract Von from his loss. With little success in placating the little victim, Rahzvon carried the wee wounded warrior to the kitchen. "Maybe you need a treat."

"Do you think it right to reward him, if he is

not behaving as you wish?" Sophia giggled. Her disapproving husband glared at her and continued toward the pantry.

One late fall afternoon, Sophia sat in their back yard beyond Urquhart, her rescued cow, with her three babies bundled up in sweaters, knitted hats and leggings. Urquhart grazed in a paddock several yards away. Each time the cow mooed, the children would laugh. It was a toss-up as to who was enjoying it more, the cow, the triplets, or their mother.

"Urquhart, what happened? You were supposed to stay small to be a pet for these three," Sophia called out.

Rahzvon sneaked up behind Sophia and kissed her neck. "Urquhart needs to grow even larger—he will make a number of fine meals for these piglets," he laughed.

"Hush, Rahzie. Do not speak of such things!" She saw the hen perched on the fence. "At least my cow has a name. Why did you not name that hen of yours?"

"She does not need one."

"You never did tell me where you got her."

"The Scots, several miles east of us."

"Oh, I remember them. She was a school teacher, at one time. What are their names?"

"His name is Donald."

"Yes, and hers is Inez."

"They had purchased her from the Ziesers."

"Dada, Dada," Ruthia interrupted. Von followed her cue while Zanya sat quietly studying a row of blocks that she assembled on the blanket.

"Hello, my little ones. Enjoying the fresh air?"

Ruthia and Von hugged his legs, until Ruthia shouted, "No, No!" and pushed her brother away from *her* father. "Mine!" she warned.

"Ruthia, we must share Daddy," Sophia explained calmly.

Ruthia wrinkled up her nose in objection and headed for her sister. She sat down next to Zanya who was meticulously adding another block to the line on the blanket. A second later and a quick swish of Ruthia's hand, the blocks were helter-skelter. Zanya did not cry or retaliate; she turned away and reached for the rope of her toy horse, mounted on the wheeled platform. Ruthia jerked it from her hand. Zanya ignored her sister and crawled off toward Urquhart.

The protective father took off after Zanya, scooped her up, and continued on to the paddock.

Secretly, hoping that he could pry one single word out of his only non-speaking child, he pointed to Urquhart.

"Cow. Can you say 'cow'? Say cow, Zanya."

To his surprise, she leaned over and whispered in her father's ear.

"Daddy, why cannot he come out and play with me?"

"Well, it is becau—"

He stopped short, wide-eyed and flabbergasted.

"Phia! Phia!!"

She jumped to her feet. "What is it?" she panicked.

"Zanya spoke to me! I was trying to get her to say 'cow' and—"

"'Tis that all?, she can say *another* word." She shook her head. "She has been saying 'mama' for a week."

"She has? But, no, Phia. You do not understand. She asked me a question in a complete sentence!"

Sophia rolled her eyes. "In this wind? You are hearing what you want to hear." She sat back down on the blanket, scrutinizing the framed photograph that she had found in the yard after the twister.

"No, Phia, she whispered it to me." He focused on Zanya. "Zanya, ask Mommy about the cow."

The indifferent little girl stared eye-to-eye with her father and then looked over his shoulder across the moors, unconcerned.

"Phia, I am telling the absolute truth!"

She stared at him blankly. "Do you think that we shall ever find the owners of this picture?"

Trina's newfound wealth remained hidden in the East wing of Hiram's home, while she and Tavy were leaving for London. Sophia took no time in insisting that the couple make inquiries about the picture, during their travel south.

"Now, be sure to stop at a minimum of two establishments in each town through which you pass," Sophia instructed.

"Sophia, Henry and I do not have a lot of extra time to devote to this search. He has to get back to the Dugans'."

"Two thirty-second conversations per town? That is hardly any time at all, considering the importance of this matter. This is serious."

Tavy smiled and shook his head. "Miss Muffet" would never change.

"We'll do our best," he cut in, "but we need to

be on our way. Please keep a close eye on Rufus. Keep him away from Hiram."

"You need not worry; Livia and I have a schedule for Rufus. He will visit with Naomi, work with Angus, go with Rahzvon on the postal route one day, play at the Wheaton's another, eat meals with Joel and, of course, attend school. He shall be so busy; he shan't notice that you are gone!"

She pulled on Trina's sleeve. Trina leaned down and Sophia whispered to her.

"Tavy is a much better match for you than Joel. You are always smiling when you are with him. Keep that in mind." This comment was followed by a wink and a wave. "Safe journey! Do not forget the photograph inquiries!"

Chapter VIII

"Helping Hand"

"And thou must count its petals well,
Because it is a gift from me;
And the last one of all shall tell
Something I've often told to thee."

—James Russell Lowell

Rufus, too, was embarking on a journey—one of new experiences and new relationships.

His visit with Naomi was anything, but uneventful. It began as a quiet afternoon. He became quickly bored with the wooden toys that Edward had retrieved from the attic—remnants from the Wheaton girls' stay at Brachney Hall. Rufus asked Naomi to teach him how to "make somethin' wi' yarn." His tiny fingers trembled, clutching the long knitting needles in a desperate attempt to maneuver the yarn.

"Do not fret Rufus. It takes patience."

She laid down her three-quarters of an infant sweater. "I think that we should take a break and have some milk and afters. Do you agree?"

Rufus glared at the uncooperative tools and nodded.

"I shall return in a few minutes. I need to give the cook instructions for the evening meal."

She left and her cat crept in. The feline leapt onto the divan and watched the guest, now pretending to sword fight with an imaginary opponent. Rufus noted his audience and grinned at it with delight.

"Aye, it takes Patience," he laughed, remembering the cat's name.

Not more than five minutes later, Naomi quickened her pace at the sound of her beloved cat's screeches emitting from the drawing room. Her jaw dropped at the sight before her. An array of yarn webbing serpentined the balusters of the staircase. On the bottom step, Patience lay bound, vocalizing her objection. Naomi's gaze flashed to the landing above where Rufus sat tapping the needles together.

Naomi screamed, "My poor kitty!" She ran to rescue her, demanding an explanation, "Rufus, how could you?"

"'Twas easy. I was the cowboy and he was the cow."

"*She!* My dear cat! Patience, Mummy is sorry!" she cried, awkwardly bending down to unwind her pet.

Edward stepped into the doorway, quite astonished to see the results of the boy's handiwork.

"This is your fault, Edward Caleb McDonnally—filling the lad's head full of cowboys and the Wild West!"

Edward glanced at the beaming culprit and said nothing. He covered his smile with his hand and went to assist his irate wife.

Naomi cuddled Patience and instructed calmly, between clenched teeth, "Rufus, go to the kitchen, and tell Angus that he is to take you, now."

"What about the afters and tea?" Rufus asked, descending the stairs.

Naomi, statue-like, did not respond. Edward took Rufus's hand. They walked to the kitchen, where Edward served him numerous scones, two glasses of milk and a cup of tea with milk. He then sent him out to find the handyman. Rufus ran to the toolshed in search of Angus.

"Afternoon, Angus!"

"Aye, Rufus. So yer here to give me a hand."

"Aye, sir."

"Verra well. We'll have to make haste. The wind's pickin' up. Ye see that shutter?"

Rufus traced his finger to the third floor

window. "Aye it doesna match the other one."

"Aye, and I need to be paintin' it. When I finish, I will lower this paint can by the rope down to ye. All ye need do is untie it and carry it carefully to the shed. Do ye understand?"

"Aye, Angus."

Rufus watched the handyman slowly work his way up the ladder, past the first floor, and then to the second. The boy was amazed to see that the "old man" had no fear to continue to the shutter above. He craned his neck to watch the shutter gradually become dark green like its pair. Angus stopped before the lower right corner was finished. The front had moved in more quickly than he had expected. The wind roared through the oaks surrounding the estate while the sky grew darker and it began to sprinkle.

"Blasted! It couldna pass o'r wi' out rainin' on me work," Angus muttered. He desperately tried to lower the pail tied to the rope, without it spilling.

He called to Rufus, "Take the pail, before the wind does!"

However, having drank those two glasses of milk and the cup of tea, Rufus had disappeared behind the shed to take care of nature's urgent call. Needless to say, the wind played havoc with the unattended pail. Naomi's hydrangea's were no longer pink, but matched the shutters perfectly.

The next morning, Sophia boosted Rufus up into the saddle behind her objecting husband.

"Phia, this is not a good idea," he whispered. "You heard what happened with Naomi and Angus."

"It will be perfectly fine. Think of all the steps

he will save you—all that dismounting and mounting. He can run up and deliver the posts for you." She looked toward the house, then back to her husband. "I know that you favor Zanya, at times, but why did you insist that she could talk?"

"Because she can."

"Oh, Rahzie," She sighed. "Now, hurry along. Here is a box of bread and cheese for you two and a thermos of milk."

"Milk? What happened to my coffee?"

"Rufus cannot drink coffee."

"Thank ye, Miss Donnally," Rufus cut in.

"*Sierzik*," Rahzvon corrected him.

"You are welcome, Rufus. Now behave."

She barely received her husband's kiss, before she ran back to the house in response to one of the infant's cries. Rahzvon squeezed the horse with his stirrups and they were off.

Sophia was partially accurate in her prediction that Rufus would save Rahzvon many steps, but she did not consider the energy needed to lift and lower the boy from the saddle. It was especially awkward with Rufus riding behind him. Halfway through the route, Rahzvon moved Rufus to the front of the saddle. Fortunately, it was a very large saddle to accommodate Mr. Kilvert so it easily allowed room for Rahzvon and the slight frame of his assistant.

Towards the end of the route, Rahzvon dismounted and lifted down his helper. They sat beneath a tree and enjoyed the treat Sophia had prepared, and the welcomed rest.

"You have been a great help to me, Rufus," Rahzvon admitted.

Rufus grinned with a mouth full of bread and

cheese. Rahzvon then offered him the milk.

Rufus drank, wiped his mouth with his sleeve and noted, "Mr. Kilbert's horse is nice, but not big like Jeanie's Pa's."

"You are right. Bruce's is a draft horse, like Hunter. There once was a horse named Sampson that would make Bruce's look like a colt standing next to him. He was over twenty-one hands tall. Mr. Wheaton's is only eighteen."

Rufus's eyes widened.

"Yes, he was a big boy. He weighed three-thousand pounds, Rufus."

Rufus looked at Mr. Kilvert's horse. "Someday, when I grow up, I can be the postman and ride Mr. Kilbert's horse. Now, that I hae been on the route."

"I am sorry, I do not think that this old boy will live that long. He is pretty old, right now. They usually only live about thirty years and he is already twenty-seven. Although I heard tell of one, named Old Billy—a famous horse who lived a lot longer. Guess how long."

Rufus rubbed his head and squinted his eyes, trying to figure the correct age.

"I would say thirty-five!"

"What would you think of sixty-two years old?"

"Whew—that is old as Mr. Donnally!"

Rahzvon grinned, "Which one?"

"Hiram, o' course."

Rahzvon burst out laughing, wishing that the middle-aged Master could have witnessed the conversation.

The two finished their snack, mounted up and headed down Margaret's Lane. Rufus sprinted to the cottage, in hopes that Rahzvon would be noting his speedy deliveries. Passing Mrs. Monroe's cottage, they saw her flying out the front door.

"Any posts for me?"

Rahzvon waved and replied, "No, Mrs. Monroe. Perhaps, next week!" She shrugged and shouted, "Fine lad, yer helper!"

"Yes, he is!" They waved at her and continued on. Rahzvon halted the horse before they reached the Huntley home.

He dismounted. "I had better deliver this one myself. I need to extend my condolences."

"What are they?"

"Mrs. Huntley lost her husband in the war. I need to tell her that I am sorry."

"Me, too." He reached for help down.

Rahzvon never imagined Rufus to be compassionate, but helped him from the saddle as requested. The two knocked and stood on the front porch waiting for her reply. She finally opened the door slowly.

"Mrs. Huntley, here is your post."

She nodded. "Thank ye Rahzvon."

Rufus stepped forward. "So sorry that Mr. Huntley isna wi' ye, but he is happy in Heaven wi' me Ma and Pa and Tavy's Ma and Pa and Jesus."

Her eyes welled up and she put her arms around him and choked out the words, "I'm grateful, lad. Thank ye."

Rahzvon added, "Yes, Sophia and I were greatly saddened to hear of Eck's passing. I feel honored to have known him. He was a good man and served his country honorably."

"Aye, there was none like me Eck. And how

are the triplets?"

"Growing like weeds and crawling...and talking," he added hesitantly.

"And who might this young man be?" she said, ruffling Rufus's hair.

Rufus grinned up at her. "Rufus McTavish."

"Tavy's young lad?" she asked looking confused.

Rahzvon clarified, "Tavy is adopting him."

"Ye are fortunate, Master McTavish. Henry is a good man. Ye mind him and make him proud."

"I will, Mum."

"Good day, Mrs. Huntley."

"Good, day."

The two mounted up and road down the lane. They had just turned up the road when Rufus broke into song.

> *"John the Smith, a fellow fine*
> *Can you shoe this horse o' mine?*
> *Yes indeed and that I can*
> *As well as any man."*

"Rahzvon?"

"Yes, Rufus."

"Was Mr. Huntley as old as Ol' Billy?"

"No, Rufus. I am sorry to say that he was several years younger."

"Me Pa, wasna verra old either. Where's yer Ma and Pa?"

"In Heaven with yours."

They finished the route early. Rahzvon dropped Rufus at the inn where the innkeeper agreed to look after him until Joel arrived.

Rahzvon shook Rufus's hand.

"You are a fine assistant. Thank you Rufus McTavish."

"Yer welcome, sir. Ye can call on me anytime, to help ye."

"I will remember that."

The next day was the most anticipated for the little traveler. He was to spend the day playing at the Wheatons' farm. Despite Maryanne's warning that the greenhouse was off limits, Rufus charmed Jeanie into believing that it would be the perfect playhouse. They sat on the dirt floor below the windows playing with her three ducks.

"What do ye want to do, now, Jeanie? I can teach ye a rhyme."

"Verra, well."

"Dan, Dan the funny grand man
Dan Dan the funny grand man
washed his face in the frying pan
combed his hair wae the leg of a chair
Dan Dan the funny grand man."

"That is all wrong," Jeanie protested. "'Tis Dan Dan funny *wee* man."

"Not the Dan I would be talkin' 'bout."

Jeanie paused and then envisioned the boisterous Daniel O'Leardon and giggled.

"Jeanie, there's a horse bigger than yer Pa's."

"I dunna believe ye."

"'Tis true. Bigger than yer house. He was named Sampson."

She looked at him skeptically.

"I wouldna be tellin' tales. Rahzvon told me."

"Are ye certain?"

"Aye, he weighed sixty-two thousand pounds!"

"That is big! I only weigh sixty-one pounds!"

"What d'ye want to do, now?"

"We could take me ducks to the pond for a swim."

"Hmm?" He looked around, studying the potted flowers on the table across from him. He jumped up, snapped off a chrysanthemum bloom, and returned to the floor next to her.

"Oh, nay! Mama will be so angry wi' ye, Rufus!"

"She'll ne'er notice. Look how many blooms on those flowers." He tucked the bloom behind the ribbon in her braid. "Bonnie, eh?"

She glanced down at it. "Aye, 'tis."

"So are ye, Jeanie."

Jeanie blushed. "Thank ye, Rufus. Come along, Shirley, Goodness and Mercy."

After a quick check to see if her mother was in the vicinity, she led the troop from the greenhouse.

"Be right along!" Rufus called. He snatched a burlap bag from beneath the table.

Chapter IX

"The Wind Blew In"

"Here take my picture; though I bid thee
farewell,
Thine, in my heart, where my soul dwells,
shall I dwell."

—John Donne

That evening Jeanie sat at the vacant table with her very distraught mother.

"Jeanie, you will be gathering eggs for the next two months."

"That is *Wilmoth's* chore."

"Not n' more. Ye pulled all the blooms from me flowers."

"Aye, Mama."

"Why?"

"Uh...to feed me ducks."

Maryanne folded her arms. "Ne'er again are ye to enter the greenhouse wi' out me."

"Aye, Mama."

"Go tend to the eggs."

Jeanie left the house carrying the egg basket. Maryanne was quite certain that her daughter was covering for Rufus. Although she had no tolerance for lying, she felt her daughter's actions were admirable.

When Jeanie entered the chicken coop, she drew out the petals from her apron pocket. She may have taken the fall, but nothing could lessen the wonder of that day with Rufus at the pond. He had made a ring of blooms around her while she sat watching her ducks enjoy their afternoon swim. She would never forget his words. "Ye are me bonnie queen, Jeanie."

Rufus spent the last couple of days with Livia. She noticed a distinct change in him since he had become Tavy's responsibility; he no longer idolized her. He was distant and reserved in her presence. Although, he was content with his new life with Tavy, he would find it difficult to ever truly forgive her. She had betrayed him from the moment Kade arrived. He held Kade equally responsible. Livia was saddened by his behavior, but understood.

Rufus was thrilled with Tavy and Trina's return. This was not the case with Sophia, for they had no news regarding the photograph. Although temporarily discouraged, Sophia decided to solicit Naomi's mystery solving abilities.

"Naomi, how are you feeling, today?" she asked.

"Ready to explode."

"You poor dear. I know. Imagine multiplying that by three."

"I cannot. But you *are* much younger."

"Yes, but you shall have a live-in nanny—an adult live-in daughter!"

"Allison may reside here, but I doubt that she will care to spend too much time caring for her baby brother or sister."

"Probably not, with Joel lurking about."

"Oh, *Sophia*... now what brings you all the way to Lochmoor Glen, today?"

She pulled the photograph from a silk bag. "This!"

"Still searching for them?"

"I am not making much headway. I thought that you may offer some methods to help."

"With whom have you spoken about it?"

"Everyone. Literally. I asked nearly everyone in the village. Trina and Tavy checked with residents in the villages on the way to Town. The results are positively depressing."

"Perhaps, you are not meant to discover its origin."

"Do not say it! Why else would it show up in my yard? Naturally, I have been chosen to find its rightful owners."

Naomi stared into Sophia's black eyes that danced with excitement. "You are determined."

"I simply have to find them. It haunts me day and night."

"Tremendous winds can send objects flying for miles."

"But it belonged in a residence. It could not have been sucked from a window; I was certain that the house must be destroyed or severely damaged."

"Sophia, have you checked any of those damaged homes?"

"Yes. Only one, besides ours, suffered any serious damage and the owners know nothing of the picture."

"It may have not been sitting in a home. It could have been from a place of business."

"The only village in proximity is Lochmoor Glen and nothing here was damaged except the pub roof."

"That was no loss. I wish it would have taken the entire building and it could have been replaced with a reputable business." Naomi thought for a moment. "It could have been stored in someone's barn."

"Only one barn other than ours was destroyed, and it was totally empty, according to the owners—except for a few sheep and a goat that thankfully, survived."

"You *have* done your research."

"I have and it has not been easy traipsing all over the countryside with the triplets. Everyone *did* enjoy meeting them though…What more can I do?"

"Is there any information on the back of the

photograph?"

Speechless, Sophia stared at the framed picture in her lap as if it were a deadly scorpion. "Quick, hand me that knitting needle!"

Naomi handed it to her. "You never took it out of the frame?" Naomi asked in sheer disbelief.

Sophia struggled to remove the back panel.

"Here, let me," Naomi insisted. She was soon lifting the panel to reveal the back of the photograph.

Sophia leaned in. "It has printing!" she squealed.

Naomi carefully removed the picture above the glass and carried it to the window.

"Well, what does it say?" Sophia demanded.

Naomi squinted and held it closer. "*No.*"

"No what?"

"*No.*" She held it up to the window. "No, I cannot believe it."

"*Naomi,* believe what?"

She handed it to Sophia whose brows knitted. "Do you—"

"Yes. I do. Alexander Mackenzie—my uncle... on my father's side...naturally."

"Your uncle is a photographer?"

"Was. He was a store dealer who then later became a photographer."

"This could have come from Grimwald, your father's home."

"No, besides, that uncle had nothing to do with Nathan." She took a seat on the divan. "Uncle Alex was born over sixty years ago in Aberdeen. He married my aunt Elizabeth. They had a parcel of bairns. Seven, I believe. They lived on... Alice Street in Bermondsey."

"What an incredible coincidence." Sophia sat in awe. She turned the picture over. "Are any of these your cousins?"

"I would not know. I met only a few of them as a small child before mother and I left Lochmoor Glen."

"This is positively perfect! We finally have a clue."

"Not really. All we know is that Uncle Alexander was the photographer."

"Perhaps he can identify them."

"Sophia, I do not know if he is still living or where he resides—if he is. And I doubt he has records of the subjects he photographed."

Sophia sighed. Oh, well... I had better be going and rescue my poor husband with our brood."

"Sophia, please leave the picture. Allow me to study it for a bit."

"Certainly. I will see myself out. Take care."

"Do not give up hope."

Naomi sat in the rocking chair, running her fingers along the edge of the portrait.

"Something seems so familiar. What is it?"

Edward came down the stairs from the bedchambers and walked over to her. "Hello, my darling magic square," he said in a low sultry tone and kissed her forehead.

"Hello darling. I was sorry to hear that Trina's inheritance was embezzled monies."

"Trina was not. In fact, she seemed sincerely relieved."

"It is a lot of responsibility—being a wealthy, independent woman. I can understand."

"*Women.* I will *never* understand. What is that

you are holding?"

"The photograph that Sophia found in their yard."

"Let me see that." He slipped it from her hand. "Who are they?"

"I have no idea, but my uncle was the photographer. It is stamped on the back."

"Small world. They must be from Lochmoor Glen. They are standing by the tree in the churchyard."

"What?!"

"Look, there's the hitching post and the cellar door."

"Edward, are you certain?" she asked anxiously, peering at the details.

"One moment." He left the room and returned with his lens. He held it over the photograph. "Yes. Indeed it's our churchyard."

"How can you tell?"

"See that?" He pointed to the hinged gate to the graveyard.

"It is the bronze angel on the gate!" she exclaimed. "Edward, you are a genius!"

"Absolutely, and do not forget it."

"We were all so busy studying the subjects that we overlooked the background. I must get word to Sophia immediately. If we only had a telephone."

"Do not start with that, again."

"Call Jules, dear."

After quite a row that evening, Sophia begrudgingly agreed to wait until morning to make the trip with her crew to Lochmoor Glen. She did not stop chattering about the picture on the entire length of the escapade.

Rahzvon dropped her at Brachney Hall, and then continued in peace to McDonnally Manor to allow the triplets to play with Kade. He and Hiram watched the children in the school play yard, but did not converse much after Rahzvon reenacted the scene on the postal route, when Rufus believed Hiram was at least sixty-two.

Sophia sat with Naomi at the library table.

"Naomi, this really narrows it down."

"Not much. We have the setting identified and know that they were acquainted with my uncle."

"Why was he here, if he lived in London? Do you think he came to visit his brother, Nathan?"

"No, as I said, they despised each other...*but* he adored... Mother!"

"Yes, dear?" Beatrice's voice resounded from the doorway.

"Mother!" Naomi attempted a quick exit from the rocker, but her additional baby weight deterred her.

"Stay seated, Baby."

"Hello! You are just the person that we needed to see!" Sophia exclaimed, holding up the picture. "It is so sweet that you still call her 'baby.' I am going to call my three 'baby' until they are old and gray."

Beatrice laughed. "Are you still trying to find the proper owners of that photograph?"

"Yes, but now we have new leads," Sophia exclaimed.

"Mother, you will never guess who the photographer is—Uncle Alexander."

"Are you serious?"

"Yes, look on the back." She did.

"How extraordinary."

Sophia gently turned it over in her hands. "Examine it. Uncle Edward recognized the details to be that of our very *own* churchyard. Do you recognize the family?"

"As I told you before, no. When was Alexander here in Lochmoor Glen?" Beatrice asked, confused.

"It is dated here in the corner," Sophia pointed out. "About twelve years ago."

"You do not think that he came to visit Nathan, do you?" Naomi asked.

"Never."

"But he favored you. Do you think that he came looking for you, Mother?"

"Possibly, but I was not here, as you know. I would have liked to have seen him. He had quite a brood with Elizabeth."

The three women sat silent.

Sophia left the divan and walked to the window. She turned and suggested, "Perhaps, he had friends travelling with him—the three in the picture."

"Perhaps," Beatrice agreed.

Sophia approached Beatrice, "Maybe you could contact him—write him a letter!" Sophia's eyes brightened.

"I suppose, if he is living in London, or living at all, I could send a note of inquiry."

"Oh, would you? I would be eternally grateful."

Beatrice laughed, "I see no harm in it, but mind you, I do not guarantee any favorable results."

"Positively, perfect! I had trouble sleeping

before I knew anything and now, the anticipation will keep me up until his reply arrives."

"Yes, thank you, Mother. Sophia has nearly lost her mind in worry over it, to the point that she barely remembers she has three bairns," Naomi giggled.

"Ah, yes, where are they, Sophia?" Beatrice asked.

"Come with me to Uncle Hiram's and Livia's and you can see them. They are crawling and talking, now. One more than the others—according to my imaginative husband."

"Hmm?" Beatrice cocked her head.

"Never mind."

Time passed ever so slowly for Sophia. Finally, the response from Alexander MacKenzie arrived. Beatrice notified Naomi, who in turn got word to Sophia.

Chapter X

"For Pete's Sake"

"To every season has our Father given
Some tokens of his love to us from heaven;
Nor leaves us here, uncheered, to walk alone,
When all we loved and prized,
in youth, has gone."

—Jones Very

In Hiram's study, Sophia read the photographer's letter aloud in Naomi's presence.

My Dear Beatrice,

I was delighted to receive your note, earlier this week. I am pleased that you are happy in your new life with the Irishman and thrilled to hear of the upcoming birth of Naomi and Edward's child.

As for the enclosed photograph, I have a bit of information. Oddly, the young boy in the picture (now a grown young man) visited with me last year.

"Where is he? Who is he?" Sophia left her chair.

"Read on," Naomi said solemnly.

Sophia finished reading the photographer's letter. She could not believe it when she read the young man's name. It said that he was now alone, as his father had passed on shortly after his mother had abandoned them. Sophia's gaze slowly rose from the letter. Her eyes welled up. "Has anyone notified his grandmother?"

"Not as yet." Naomi shook her head. "I thought that since you discovered the photograph. Well...it is bittersweet."

Sophia studied the photograph. "Yes, her son is gone, but her grandson is well. He is about my age." She carefully placed the photograph in the silk bag. "I must go and tell her. Could you, please, tell Rahzvon that I shall be back, shortly.

He is out at the fountain with the children...He said that she was always waiting for a letter," she mumbled.

"I'll tell him." Naomi gave her a hug. "I'll have Miles get you a carriage."

"No. I would rather walk."

Naomi nodded.

With a heavy heart, Sophia lifted her wrap from the hall tree. This would be one of the most difficult visits that she would ever make. Preoccupied with how she would present her discovery, she walked mechanically down the road. It was a delicate matter, which needed to be handled gently and compassionately.

The sign, *Margaret's Lane,* loomed overhead. Clutching the picture, she took a breath and entered the lane. She stepped upon the first flagstone leading to the Monroe cottage door. She closed her eyes. Her moment of silent prayer suddenly ended by the pounding of approaching hooves on the cobblestones. A young man riding a beautiful, black horse stopped next to her.

Sophia ran all the way back to the McDonnally mansion. Beaming-ear-to-ear, she raced down the main corridor shouting, "Where is everyone?"

Eloise peeked from the kitchen. "We are in here!"

She flew into the kitchen, breathless and exhausted. "It was an honest-to-goodness fairytale come to life!"

Naomi, Livia, and Beatrice left their chairs to join Eloise while Sophia balanced herself with a hand on the ladder-back chair.

"There I was, on the path to the Monroe cottage and he rode up, *right* beside me!"

"Who?" Naomi asked impatiently.

"Him! The grandson! Adam Monroe!"

"Mrs. Monroe's?" Beatrice asked.

"Yes! The moment I saw him, I recognized the similarity with the lad in the picture. In fact, upon seeing him, I immediately looked to the picture."

"I can only imagine how thrilled she was to see him." Eloise said, wiping away a tear with the corner of her apron.

"It was heart-wenching." Sophia sighed.

"*Wrenching*," Naomi carefully corrected her.

"No matter, my heart was breaking. It was the most uplifting experience since the triplets were born!" She glanced at Livia. "Of course, not that your wedding was not exhilarating. But there they were, embracing the stuffings out of one another—crying and laughing all at the same time! Naturally, I felt that I was interfering, but Adam asked me to stay."

"Why had he waited so long to see her?" Naomi asked, sitting back down at the table.

"I do not know. All I know is that he came to Lochmoor Glen after his visit with Alexander Mackenzie. En route, the twister hit. My twister! It hit the bothy where he took cover from the storm. His saddlebag holding the picture was sucked away. Then he was further delayed by the loss of his horse."

Sophia took a seat in the chair. "And that was that. Grandmother and grandson reunited in time for Christmas, all because of my finding the photograph in my yard," she said, grinning with victory.

The women looked at one another curiously thinking, *not exactly*.

Naomi asked, "Sophia, I thought that you spoke to *everyone* in Lochmoor Glen about the picture."

"I did. Well, almost everyone. I guess I did not believe that any of Uncle Hiram's tenants had the means to pay a photographer. I did not consider their kin, I suppose."

"I guess you learned to never assume, as so many here in our village have," Beatrice teased.

Ignoring her comment, Sophia looked over the plate of cookies that Eloise was placing on the table. "They look delicious." She graciously took three.

Harriet Dugan's Christmas gift presented the Dugan family with a number of problems, other than being stalled away from Jock and needing his own source of fresh water. Having been removed from his warmer climate, Pete arrived unprepared for the winter months. That became quite apparent the evening when Joseph blasted in through the backdoor.

"Harriet, ye hae to do somethin'! Yer wee donkey is shiverin' and shakin'!"

"Put him in thestall wi' Jock!" she said, focused on the loaves of bread that she was kneading at the kitchen table.

"Nay, I told ye he canna go in there. He and Jock dunna care for one anot'er."

"They will hae to get o'er it."

"Be reasonable Harriet."

"'Tis yer problem. Ye should hae thought 'bout it, before ye had Tavy fetch it."

"Ma, 'tis serious. He's young—we may lose him."

She dropped the dough to the table. "What do ye want me to do? Go put that old horse blanket on him," she grumbled.

"'Tis too big and filthy. Rufus used it as a sled behind Jock—through the muddy field."

"I'm not washin' it, Joseph Dugan!"

"There's n' time for that. Yer good wi' a needle and thread, ye could make him one."

She glared at him. "Do ye not think that I hae better things to do than make a donkey ganzer?"

"Harriet, if ye dunna make him a coat o' sorts, I will be bringin' him in here, where 'tis warm!"

"Ye dare not!"

"I do, so ye hae better get sewin'!" He stormed out.

She scrunched the dough with her angry fists, ripped it in two, and tossed them into the greased pans.

"Always somethin'! That beast 'tis not me gift, 'tis me burden!"

She stood with her hands planted on her hips. She considered the possibility of her stubborn husband having the nerve to bring that animal into her clean kitchen. She peered out the window. Joseph had wrapped *his* coat around the little donkey.

"Uh," she sighed. She headed for the cellar, went directly to the steamer trunk, and flipped the latches. There on top lay the plaid wool blanket that she had lined with sheepskin for her late dog, Angel. She lifted it, noting the large hole, chewed from the middle.

"Ye rascal," she laughed.

She folded it, closed the lid, and returned upstairs. She checked out the window. There her husband stood in the barn, in his ganzer, holding a rope to the outside where the donkey stood, sporting Joseph's coat. She shook her head, continued into the front room, and spread the blanket out on the floor. She removed her pair of scissors, two large black buttons, a black ribbon, a heavy needle and a spool of darning thread. She sat them on the end table next to her armless sewing rocker. Gripping her paper tape measure, she pulled her shawl over her shoulders and headed outside.

Exactly eighteen minutes later, Harriet carried the finished product to the back porch and motioned for Joseph to lead Pete to the fitting room. She placed the blanket across the donkey's back and pulled its tail through the loop adorned with a black bow. She wrapped the neckpiece around Pete's neck and buttoned it. A perfect fit. Joseph could not stop smiling, as she reached under Pete's belly and tied the two bands.

"There," is all that she said and disappeared into the house.

Joseph petted Pete's forehead. "Ye see, laddie, yer Ma loves ye."

On extra cold days, Pete wore his coat proudly. However, one extremely cold, snowy day, Rufus shot into the house.

"Mrs. Dukan, Mrs. Dukan! Ye hae to do somethin'!"

Harriet who was chatting with Eloise in the living room, jumped from her chair.

"What is it lad? Is it Joseph or Tavy? Are they

hurt?" she panicked.

"Nay!" He shouted back. She rushed to the kitchen to see him grabbing Joseph's muffler.

"What has happened lad?" she demanded.

"'Tis Pete."

"What has he done, now?"

"Nothin', 'tis his ears. They are freezin'!"

"What do ye expect? They are bigger than a hare's! Wait a minute, lad—what are ye doin' wi' Pa's muffler?"

"I need it for Pete!"

"For Mercy's sake, Rufus, I gave that to him for Christmas. I paid a pretty penny for that yarn!"

"If only a penny, ye can buy some more!" Dragging the scarf, he ran from the room.

She caught him by the collar. "Hang up that muffler, lad, now! Eloise! I'll be wi' ye in a minute!" she shouted.

"Aye, Mum, but—"

"Out wi' ye!"

Rufus, started outside, grumbling:

"Cross patch, lift the latch
Sit by the fire and spin;
Take a cup and drink it up
Then call your neighbor's in!"

"Who would ye be callin' a cross patch?" Harriet bellowed.

That afternoon, Pete pranced contently around the pasture donning his new coat and shirtsleeve earmuffs, held in place at the crown by Angel's old dog harness.

That evening at the supper table, Tavy looked

at Harriet. "Ma, yer a wonder, outfittin' Pete. But, he doesna like the snow. He could use some boots."

She glared silently over her teacup. That was the last straw. Two pairs of children's boots from the mercantile sufficed.

It was not long before Adam Monroe was found to be quite sociable; he made every effort to meet each of the Lochmoor Glen residents. Shortly after his arrival, he called on the members of the Brachney Hall estate. He was no sooner invited in, when the butler, Jules, was called away to the kitchen. The cook was shrieking about a roast set ablaze.

After several minutes, Mr. Monroe took a seat on the Deacon's bench where he waited to be announced. He could not help but overhearing the conversation of the two women in the adjoining room.

"Mother, I cannot understand it. Men are so incredibly different than us."

"True. They are in many ways, but similar in some. It is all in a matter of degrees and situation, I believe."

"Degrees?"

"For example: men demonstrate a great degree of instability and emotion when cast into an unfamiliar situation. One such would be childbearing. Men tend to go all to pieces when a woman is about to deliver. However, given a discussion of motorcars or finance, if that is their expertise, they remain in control, unless their ego is attacked. Then they fly off the handle."

Naomi continued, "Now, on the other hand,

women such as ourselves, when we are met with an unfamiliar situation, listen, learn, and absorb the information and act accordingly. In an emergency, we handle it calmly, graciously, without faltering. And women tend to challenge derogatory rumor or accusations with keen logic and simply deny its justification."

"Yes, yes we do! And men are so terribly fickle."

"To whom are you referring?"

"Hiram, of course and his many women," she said snidely.

"Yes, Hiram is a difficult sort, but Allison, he did find his perfect match."

"And what about Guillaume? First he is with Trina, then me, and now, Mercy. And Joel...well he's so unpredictable."

"You know that Joel cares for you."

Jules returned to the patient guest and apologized for the delay. He led him to the drawing room.

"Madame McDonnally, Miss O'Connor, I present Adam Monroe."

Adam smiled broadly, focused on the beautiful young Allison.

"Welcome to Brachney Hall, Mr. Monroe." Naomi awkwardly pushed herself up from the rocker.

"No need to get up. I was in the neighborhood and felt it a necessity to introduce myself to two of the most *gracious, calm,* controlled and I might add, lovely women in the village."

The two looked nervously at one another.

"No need to panic ladies, to any *degree.* I am merely a helpless, out-of-control male who may *fly off the handle* at any given minute, so dare not challenge *my ego.*"

Naomi and Allison sat speechless, not knowing whether to be embarrassed or outraged. He looked to Patience, stretched out on the couch next to Allison. "Got their tongues?" he addressed the purring cat. He then laughed at the sight of their bewildered expressions.

"My dear ladies, do you not believe in what you profess to be true of the weaker sex? I must go. The pleasure was all mine. I have several more visits to make—which may be my *expertise.* Good day." He nodded and was gone.

Allison turned to her mother, but knew not what to say. Finally, Naomi mumbled, "Unpredictable."

Allison sat awestruck and only gave a slight shrug.

While visiting the other McDonnally mansion, Adam met the visiting Sierzik family. Rahzvon and Adam hit it off from the start. From that day forward, Mr. Monroe accepted the weekly invitation to dine with the Sierziks. Rahzvon welcomed the male companionship of the newest resident; Guillaume and Tavy were both preoccupied with their social lives. He enjoyed the hours conversing with a peer; a temporary diversion from his fatherly duties. Sophia took advantage of this new relationship, as well.

Early one afternoon, Sophia joined the two men sitting on the newly built porch. After a minute, she got up.

"Well, gentlemen, since you two are content to sit here and chat, I am certain that you will have no objection to my taking a stroll around the *grounds*, as Rahzie calls them. The children are napping."

"No, Phia. Go right ahead," Rahzvon said cheerily.

"You are an angel," she said, kissed his forehead, and sauntered around the side of the house.

"Quite a wife, you have, Rahzvon."

"She's more than any man could expect. Good mother, decent cook, fairly good housekeeper, great—"

The wagon that went racing past the house interrupted him.

"Bye Rahzie, Adam! See you in a few hours. Meeting Allison!"

The irate husband flew from his chair. "That conniving little—"

"More than any man could expect?" Adam laughed.

.

Chapter XI

"The Legacy"

"That to the world are children
Through them it feels the glow
Of a brighter and sunnier climate
Though reaching the trunks below."

—Henry Wadsworth Longfellow

About half way between the Sierzik home and Lochmoor Glen was the tiny village of Wemyss—population nineteen. No one was certain if it was named for the Wemyss clan or for the large cave it was built around (wemyss meaning "cave"). The village offered little, but was the home of a pub that was famous for its sandwiches. This is where Sophia asked Allison to meet with her. Their relationship ran hot and cold, but today, they were best of friends.

Allison arrived only a few minutes after Sophia was seated at one of the three vacant booths.

"Hello, Allison."

"Good afternoon, Sophia. I see that you successfully made your Saturday getaway."

"Went like clockwork."

"Nice sailor blouse."

"Thank you. They are very popular right now. What do you think of the new military style suits with the applets and capes?"

Allison smoothed her skirt. "A bit too masculine for me. I prefer the layered flowing skirts, like this." She left the booth to show off the smart suit embellished with embroidered Chinese medallions adorning the waist and sleeves.

"Very posh."

"Thank you. So what is the urgent news?" she asked, returning to her seat.

Sophia leaned forward. "You, my dear, are in a doubly delightful dilemma!"

"What dilemma?"

"The attention of two men—every woman's dream! The choice is yours!"

"First of all, having the affections of two men

could be anything but delightful. It could be exasperating and confusing. Secondly, I have no idea of which two men you are speaking," she said coyly and picked up her menu.

"Do not pretend to be naïve with me, Allison O'Connor. Joel Merriman and Adam Monroe."

"Adam Monroe?" She swallowed hard.

"Surely you are aware that the man is obsessed with you."

"Obsessed? I only met the man once and never spoke a word to him."

"Yes, he talks about you all the time. He visits frequently and is forever asking questions about you and his opponent, Joel."

"Opponent? Yes, Joel and I are seeing each other. But he only calls on me once a week."

"Excuse me," the owner interrupted, "but what would ye be carin' to order today?"

"I will have the beef," Allison ordered.

"Beef? Oh, I could not—not with Urquhart. I'll have the chicken. I have no feelings for Rahzie's hen."

The owner nodded with squinted eyes. "Hmm."

"And two teas, please," Sophia added. He took the menus and left to the kitchen.

"They may even have a duel over you," Sophia said casually.

"Duel? Do not be absurd. I barely know the man."

"It may be a case of love at first sight, like Rahzie and me. You have to admit that it is terribly exciting!"

"But, Mr. Monroe is—"

"Mr. Monroe is what? Do not tell me that you

do not find him to be appealing because of his injury! It is only a damaged muscle in his leg."

"Well, I—"

"Allison O'Connor, I am ashamed of you. You—daughter of Naomi, who has lived her life, without any regard to the scar on her face, you— you are judging poor Adam—marking him as inferior because of an insignificant wound that he received honorably in battle, and I might add, has no bearing on his personality!"

"Sophia, stop!"

The owner placed the sandwiches and teacups on the table. "Please, lower yer voices. I may be gettin' more patrons any minute."

"So sorry, sir," Sophia apologized and rolled her eyes, knowing it was highly unlikely any customers would appear that late in the afternoon.

"Verra well. Now keep it down."

"Allison, I only recently finished reading *Of Human Bondage* and that poor man suffered a club foot and treachery from a horrible waitress! But he became a physician and met Sally and lived happily ever after!"

"Enough! I am not any less interested in Mr. Monroe because of his injury. I simply do not know anything about him, except that he is incredibly rude and insolent."

"Adam? Are we speaking of the same man? Allison, you are in for a very pleasant surprise. Why, if I had not fallen in love with Rahzie, married him, and had our beautiful babies, I would not think twice about considering Adam. He is funny, polite, and loves children." She picked up her sandwich, "Do not be so quick to make up your mind. You have not agreed to marry Joel."

She took a bite.

"No...but I think that he shall propose, soon."

Sophia nearly choked. "Allison this is a serious commitment! You have to be certain. What would be a better way to gauge your feelings for Joel, than by becoming acquainted with Adam? It will do no harm."

"I believe that Joel will beg to differ with you."

Sophia returned home to find it topsy-turvy, in utter chaos, and emitting a variety of sounds. Von and Ruthia were fighting over a stuffed giraffe, Rahzvon was screeching about her absence, while sweating over a pot of boiling baby bottles, and Zanya was giggling, listening to Adam read *Pollyanna Grows Up.*

"I am back!" she called, laying her pocket book on the top shelf, above the coat hooks.

Adam left his chair, toting Zanya. He moved quickly to her side. "What did she say?"

"Hello, Zanya." She kissed her forehead. She glanced at Adam. "Allison really had no idea that you had any interest in her."

"Phia, come in here, now!"

"One moment, dear!"

"So did she respond favorably?" Adam asked eagerly.

"There is a matter of she and Mr. Merriman—but I insisted that she consider all of her options before making any drastic decisions."

"He has proposed?" he asked, concerned.

"No, not as yet. But I feel that you had better make your move without haste."

"Phia! Come tend to these bottles...please!"

Adam was satisfied with the outcome of the

meeting. He nodded with approval. "I shall—and she will not know what hit her."

"Phia!"

"Coming, Love!"

Mr. Monroe began his campaign to win the affections of the beautiful Miss O'Connor. He returned to his grandmother's cottage, armed with a grand plan.

"Hello, Gramroe," he said, rushing past her on the flagstone path; "Gramroe" being the nickname, for Grandma Monroe which he called her as a child.

She started to greet him, but instead went about weeding between the stones in seeing his haste. He entered the tiny room that she had prepared for him on the day of his arrival. There was only enough walking space between the bureau and the bed. A single chair sat under the one window. It was a small room, but adequate. He pulled open the top drawer of the bureau, removed a cloth bag, and dumped the contents on to the coverlet. He carefully examined each of the three, under the curious scrutiny of his grandmother, who stood unnoticed in the doorway.

All three were carved identically. Each was sanded smooth to the touch. He carried them to the window and stood them on the sill in their proper order. He folded his arms and nodded with approval when he felt his grandmother's hand on his shoulder.

"So ye hae found her—the One."

"Yes."

"I am happy for ye. 'Tis good to see 'em, again.

I remember the day that yer grandfather presented 'em to me." She took a seat in the chair. "The rain had stopped and I was sittin' on a bench in Holyrood Park. I was watchin' the birds splashin' in the puddles. They were havin' a grand time. Then a young man stepped between me and the birds. He was tall like ye."

"Grandfather?"

"Nay, 'twas John Reid—a young man I was courtin'. He asked if I wouldna care to take a stroll wi' him. I said, 'nay.' I knew what he had on his mind."

"What was that, if I may ask?" he teased.

"To propose."

"So you were avoiding him?"

"Aye, I felt n' sparks wi' him. He was taken aback by me refusal and left. I sat for a bit longer and noticed a man watchin' me. A man wi' a friendly smile and warm eyes, like yers."

"Grandfather."

"Nay, but yer grandfather was standin' next to him. Oh, what a fine figure o' a man. He was big and brawny, but had a gentle face. They talked a bit, then the other man left. Yer grandfather walked straight over to me. All he said was, 'Me name is Nicholas Monroe.' Then he handed the cloth bag to me." She picked it up from the bed. "This verra one." She stared at it for a minute, seeming lost in the memory.

"He then disappeared. Me hands were tremblin'. I didna hae any idea 'bout what was in the bag. I remember—I was shocked, but thrilled. After, that day, me whole world changed. I was changed."

"How long before you were married?"

"Six months to the day."

Adam took her hand in his and patted it. She left the chair. He put his arm over her shoulders and the two regarded the three statues standing nobly in the sunlight in the window.

"Gramroe, why is it that Grandfather gave them to me, instead of Pa?"

"Adam 'tis no secret that yer parents' marriage 'twas not a good one. When yer father brought yer mother home to meet us, your grandfather wasna pleased wi' his choice. It was too late for the gift. I will say n' more."

She laid the bag back on the bed. "Yer Grandfather had hopes that ye would find the right woman."

"I have. I knew it was her, the moment I heard her voice."

"What did she say?"

"She was in the other room speaking highly critically of men," he said, grinning.

"Aye?" The grandmother grimaced.

"Then I met her and she was more beautiful than I ever imagined, but I knew by her voice that she had to be extraordinary."

"Might ye share the name o' this outspoken angel?"

"Angel she is. Allison O'Connor."

His grandmother did not respond.

"Gramroe, do you know her? What am I saying? Of course, you do."

"Aye, she is verra bonnie, but…"

"But what?"

"She's a McDonnally."

"Yes, she is. Now, I must deliver these immediately." He snatched up the bag and carefully placed them in it in their proper order. "Like you, she has another suitor—the schoolmaster. But she'll be mine. I have to go," he said, pulling the drawstrings on the bag. He kissed her cheek. "I shall be back shortly, Gramroe!"

"Dunna be late! We're havin' finnan toasties and powsowdie!"

She stood at the window watching him mount up and ride off.

"Miss O'Connor?" She shook her head.

Adam was elated at the prospects of presenting the magical gift. His black horse delivered him to Brachney Hall in record time. He tied it outside and rapped the doorknocker. Jules answered.

"I am here to see Miss O'Connor, sir. Could you please, have someone cool down my horse?"

"Of course, sir. but I am sorry to report that Miss O'Connor is otherwise engaged."

The word "engaged" sent up a red flag. "But I have to see her!"

"Sir, she is entertaining a guest."

"Then I shall have to wait."

He stepped passed Jules and took the familiar seat on the deacon's bench in the hall.

"Sir, this is highly irregular. She may not be available to see you for...for hours."

"I shall wait."

Adam sat privy to the giggles and laughter of his intended and his nemesis Joel. The wait was not a pleasant one, but he refused to be discouraged because he held the magic; he had a tight grip on the cloth bag. His hands began to sweat while the playful banter continued.

Jules was in a precarious situation—not knowing if he should alert Miss O'Connor to the guest's presence, or to leave her and Mr. Merriman undisturbed, as instructed. The butler was overcome with deja vous. Miss O'Connor had a habit of leaving men unattended in the front hall. After forty-five long minutes, Jules made his move and prayed it was the right choice. He entered the drawing room.

"Excuse me, Miss O'Connor. I need to have a private word with you."

"What is it? I asked to not be disturbed," she said annoyed.

Jules looked over his shoulder at the beaming caller, parked on the bench. Her eyes widened.

"He is waiting to speak with you. He has waited quite a while."

"How long?" she whispered.

"Forty-five minutes," he said in a soft tone.

"I am obviously very busy. Ask him to leave."

"I did. He refuses. He wishes to wait."

She peeked around Jules and glanced at the handsome guest, now standing. She walked over to Joel who was examining his fingernails.

"Joel, I have some urgent business to which I need to attend. You do not mind, do you?"

He placed his hands on her shoulders. "Not at all, love. We are still dining tonight?"

"Yes, yes."

"Until later. I will be counting the seconds."

"Good afternoon, Joel."

Joel left, albeit reluctantly when he saw the all too good-looking "business" towering over him.

Allison instructed Jules to invite in the guest.

She scurried to the divan, sat as proper as possible, and then moved immediately to the safety of the rocking chair.

Adam walked in. She was surprised that once again, she was frazzled by his appealing appearance.

He stood in front of her, smiling.

"My name is Adam Monroe," he said proudly.

"I know. We have met."

The smile fell from his face. Would this kill the magic? He quickly handed her the bag. Bowed from the waist and left abruptly.

She was left holding the bag in mid-air with mouth open, at a loss for words, *again*. He had waited forty-five minutes for this?

She jumped from the chair and ran to the window. He was riding away. She held the bag up like a dead fish, walked hesitantly back to the divan and sat down.

She eyed the gold drawstrings and nervously glanced around the room.

"Hmm."

She pulled them apart and peeked inside. She squinted curiously and cautiously pulled out the top one. It was a beautifully carved bear, standing on all fours about the size of her palm. It was lacking in detail—tiny ears and legs beneath its rounded body.

On its right side, there were inscribed words of gold.

"Bear with me."

She half smiled, reached into the bag and pulled out the next. It was identical to the first, but reading: "I bearly know you" on its back.

She giggled a little and quickly withdrew the

last one. She turned the bear over to its left side.

"But I cannot bear life without you."

She bit her bottom lip, and then smiled as she had never smiled before.

She leaned back. "Adam Monroe."

Adam joined his grandmother at the supper table and they bowed their heads.

"Oh thou who kindly dost provide
For ev'ry creatures want.
We bless the God of Nature wide
For all Thy goodness lent.
And if it please Thee, heavenly Guide
May never worse be sent;
But whether granted or denied,
Lord bless us with content."

Mrs. Monroe ladled the powsawdie, smoked haddock in sheep's head broth, into Adam's bowl. "Hae the three bears found a new home?"

"Temporarily."

"I made cabbie-claw, if ye prefer it to the toasties."

"Haddock, cod—I love it all and Miss O'Connor, too."

She offered a brief grin. "Will ye hold the ladder, while I lime-wash up along the roof, tomorrow?"

"Dear Gramroe, I am in such a grand mood I'll lime wash the entire cottage myself. You can sit and watch and look beautiful."

"Adam, ye silly lad," she giggled.

The three bears stood on the side table,

overseeing the Brachney Hall drawing room. Edward, an avid stamp collector and aficionado of detail was the first to spot them. He picked each one up and read the inscriptions. A smile crept across his face. He returned them to their appropriate order and continued upstairs. Naomi entered the room a few minutes later and walked past the guardians without initially noticing them. She entered the staircase. She paused and withdrew her right foot from the first step; she walked back to the end table where the new inhabitants were posted.

"What do we have here?" she murmured, picking up one of the three wooden creatures. "Could they be Joseph's carvings?"

She read the inscription and returned it to the table. She repeated the process with the remaining two.

"Well, they are not a gift from Edward. We have known each other for years. Must be for Allison...from Joel. How sweet." She returned to the staircase and continued upstairs.

That evening Mr. Merriman arrived at Brachney Hall at six-thirty to escort Allison to supper. Jules invited him to wait in the parlor where he scanned the furnishings, then took a seat on the divan. He was reaching for a copy of *Punch* when the three bears caught his eye.

"What's this?" He turned the first over in his palm and then the remaining two.

"Good evening, Joel," Naomi greeted. She entered from the hall. "How awfully clever and thoughtful of you, to present those adorable carvings to my daughter."

"Joel, I am ready," Allison interrupted behind her mother.

"Your mother is under the impression that I gave you these primitive pieces," he said disapprovingly.

Allison glanced at the bears. "She was mistaken...shall we go?"

"But where did they come from?" her always curious mother inquired.

"Yes, where?" Joel demanded.

"Mr. Monroe brought them," she said bluntly.

"Monroe? I should have suspected. The man cannot even spell."

"What?" Naomi said, examining the three in question.

"If you will take note. On the first, 'barely' is misspelled."

"Joel," Allison cut in, "I believe it is a clever play on words, being bears."

"No matter. It should have been written correctly. What a simpleton," he snickered. "Shall we go?" he smiled, offering her his arm.

Allison stood firm. Naomi glanced nervously around the room and made a quick exit.

"Good evening, Mr. Merriman," Allison said sharply and followed her mother out.

Chapter XII

"In a Word"

"I have you fast in my fortress
And will not let you depart,
But put you down into the dungeon
In the round-tower of my heart."

—Henry W. Longfellow

Trina and Tavy rode down the road toward the village enjoying the gentle breeze and the first glimmer of twilight. The sun had set and a full moon glowed brightly above them.

"Henry, will you write to me, while you are serving at Shueburyness?"

"I am not much for correspondin', but I shall, now and again."

"It should be terribly interesting work. I love dogs. They are so very good-natured, as a rule."

"The dogs at the training center are soldiers—trained to ignore people and keep their minds on their work. They..."

Seeing Guillaume and Mercy sharing a bench on the green, distracted him. They were laughing and conversing. Tavy, fixated on the jovial couple, halted the horse.

"Henry?" Trina touched his arm.

He did not respond. He sat silent, deaf to her comment. He then snapped the reins and drove off.

The laughter ceased. "I shall miss you terribly, Guillaume," Mercy said shyly.

Guillaume placed his arm around her shoulders.

"Not to worry, Mercy, I shall write to you. What shall we do to celebrate, when this horrid conflict ends? Shall we pool our resources and purchase the Virgin Islands and move there for a life of luxury and peace?" he teased.

"Not possible. The United States bought them for twenty-five million."

"More the pity, but I do prefer the British Isles. Perhaps a picnic and some salmon fishing on the River Dee or some trout fishing in the West Highland? Are you game, Mercy? You do like to fish?"

Mercy looked across the green at Tavy's disappearing wagon. *Like to fish? Naturally.* She had hoped to marry a fisherman at one time. She quickly changed the subject.

"I may have to join the suffragist movement. It is an international concern, now."

"Well, do not write to me that you are behind bars, like those women that were arrested at the White House in Washington, or that you have thrown yourself under the royal carriage," he warned with a half-smile.

"Well, renown suffragist, Emily Dawson, wrote no one after that courageous demonstration. And to think that she was denied a Christian burial...When are you leaving?"

"In a few days."

"Have you spoken to Tavy about riding with him to the school?"

"Not as yet. He has been distancing himself from me."

Guillaume and Tavy reported for duty at the dog training center. They did not travel together, nor did they acknowledge one another, other than an occasional nod.

One morning at the post call, the two men stood a few yards apart.

"McDonnally!"

Guillaume stepped forward to retrieve three envelopes. He chuckled to himself. "Oh, *Mercy.*"

"McTavish!"

Tavy raised his hand and took the letter

bearing Trina's handwriting. He watched Guillaume excitedly opening the envelopes, stuffed Trina's into his trouser pocket, and walked back to the barracks.

Agnes Murray sat on the swing hanging from the mammoth oak tree on the north side of her family's home. She carefully slid her finger under the flap of the soil-stained envelope. She took a breath and removed the letter:

Me sweet Agnes,

'Tis me greatest pleasure receiving your letters. They are probably the only thing that assures me that there is another world outside these trenches. So, Guillaume and Tavy have gone to Shueburyness to train the war dogs and are spared this hell. Those pups are a Godsend delivering messages over four-thousand meters, behind the lines.

Sorry to hear about the loss of the O'Leardon children in Quay. Tell Daniel, I send my condolences to his cousin. The Irish/English battle is another war that needs to end. Both are taking the lives of too many—too many children. I was not going to tell ye, but since it is in the past, I am of the few that was not injured or perished at Somma. 'Twas a soldiers worse nightmare.

Thank Rahzvon, again, for helping Pa with the postal route. I have heard that he is one of the few postal carriers not riding sidesaddle! I canna imagine him with the triplets. He had his hands full with Sophia. Hopefully, we shan't be triply blessed with our first!

Maybe the second, after we have had some practice with one bairn.

I cannot believe that Bat Masterson—gunman, buffalo hunter was appointed U.S. Marshall by President Roosevelt. I would wager that Edward is thrilled. The west may remain wild!

I will end this now, with my heart aching, as I hold your tattered photograph. I love you and pray that we will be together by next Christmas. Pray for a truce!

> *Your ever-loving future husband,*
> *Jake*

Several more residents were now joining the armed forces, since the Bachelor Bill had passed. Joel Merriman was not an exception. He stood on the steps of McDonnally Manor donning his army uniform. Hiram held Kade with one arm—his other securely around Livia.

Joel smiled at her. "Do not worry about the school. It is in good hands."

"Joel, I am not a certified teacher."

"Livia, you are as qualified as any. With the detailed curriculum that I left for the older students, and the suggestions that I made for the younger children, I feel certain that all will run quite smoothly. You are quite capable of creating a syllabus for the younger pupils. I am sorry to leave you with so much responsibility, so abruptly. Feel free to contact my London colleague, whom I spoke of. He will be available to address any problems, if any, that may arise."

"I will do my best until you return."

"I am confident that the students shall not suffer in the slightest with my absence."

Hiram cleared his throat.

"Merriman...our relationship has been strained at times, but you take my prayers for your safe return."

"Thank you, Mr. McDonnally and, again, I thank you for your contribution of your home for the school—even if it was offered under duress," he laughed.

Hiram removed his arm from Livia's shoulders and extended his hand. "Good Luck, ol' man."

"Thank you, sir."

Livia, barely able to speak, said with melancholia, "Joel, please keep us informed. Write to us."

"I will."

In the far pasture behind the Dugan cottage, Rufus sat astride the little donkey, Pete. Mercy, en route to the Stewarts', saw him and headed through the meadow.

"Hello, Rufus."

He did not turn at her greeting. She walked around Pete. Rufus looked up with tear-filled eyes.

"Oh, sweet boy, do not worry. Tavy will be fine. This is something that he must do. He has no other choice.

"Why?" Rufus sniffled.

"There has been a new law passed—a rule that all unmarried men, Tavy's age and older, must serve in the military—to help with the war. But Rufus, he will not be in harm's way. He is fortunate to have the opportunity to work with the war dogs, like Guillaume. Did Tavy not tell you this?"

"Some of it. If my pa married you, could he come back?"

She was speechless.

"Ye said married men can stay home."

"No, no...he is a bachelor. Besides, he and Trina—"

"But he loves ye, Miss Mercy."

"*Rufus.*"

"'Tis true. I heard him tellin' me grandfather Joseph, before he left."

"No, no you misunderstood."

"Yer name is Mercy, is it not?"

"Yes."

Rufus nodded.

Sophia sat in the parlor with her mother, Hannah, watching the triplets play.

"Mother, thank you for coming today to help with the babies. Without a nanny, I barely have time to cook and clean."

"It is my pleasure. It keeps my mind busy, without fearful thoughts of Oscar."

"Mother, why did you not marry him? Then he could have stayed."

"The bill was passed and that was that. It is ironic that his forty-first birthday was only a few months ago. I have to believe that it was God's will that we were not to marry, as yet. Perhaps, he will save the lives of his fellow soldiers."

"Or, God wanted you to have this time with your grandbabies."

"The triplets are my salvation and your home is my sanctuary." She smiled at the toddlers

moving about the room. "Pray for him, Sophia."
"I will Mama—every night."

Chapter XIII

"To a Great Degree"

"The ideal husband understands
every word his wife doesn't say."

—Alfred Hitchcock

Naomi rocked gently, knitting her fourth pair of booties. Edward lowered *The English Review* and looked over the top of his glasses at her busily clicking needles.

"A blue pair this time?"

"Yes, I finished the green, yellow and white pairs. Edward, what girl's name do you prefer?"

"Is it not customary to name her after your mother?"

"Beatrice? But darling, that is my middle name."

"It is?"

"Oh, *Edward*."

"Well, then use Beatrice's middle name."

"Do you really want a daughter named Smithfield?"

"Certainly. We could call her Smitty," he laughed.

"Very amusing. We need a name—we have not much time."

"Dearest, give us a son and we shan't have this dilemma."

Naomi stopped rocking. "We could name her after your mother, Catherine."

"We could...or we could use her middle name."

"What is that? I cannot remember."

"Norton. Norton Smitty McDonnally—it has a nice ring to it. Darling, no man could resist a woman with a name like that." He hid behind his paper.

"Edward Caleb McDonnally, you would do anything to deter gentleman callers from our doorstep."

He dropped his paper into his lap. "Do you

blame me? Look at my history with our first. Why everyone has been on the prowl for Allison—George Hicks, Guillaume—even Hiram—both nephews! Now Joel and his bears and—"

"Those bears are not from Joel. Besides, have you not heard? Allison ended that only a few days before he joined the army."

"Joel, in the army?"

"Yes, he is leaving today."

"But who gave her the bears?"

"Adam Monroe."

"Now Adam, too?"

"So, what of it? Allison is quite a catch and attracts many moths to the flame."

"I should daresay her baby sister shall be quite as beautiful—you *are* her mother. My troubles shall never end."

"You are absolutely right, dear. I shall give you a son to save you the trouble." She continued with her knitting.

After a few minutes, she dropped the unfinished bootie into her lap.

"Edward, since the English/Irish conflict at Quay, I have been worried about Mother and Daniel."

"I cannot predict what he will do—nearly four-hundred civilians killed—forty children at the Primary School—one of his own clan. He is very angry; there is no doubt about that."

"Mother should not have gone to Dublin with him. I am afraid for her."

"Not to worry—Daniel will look out for her. She is the love of his life."

"His family would have understood her absence at the funeral."

"Dear, Beatrice felt that she needed to be there with him. You would have done the same."

"Yes, yes, I would have."

"They should be coming home soon. Try not to dwell on it and know that they are in God's hands."

"Yes, dear, I shall try." She tied off a row.

Edward turned the page of the newspaper.

"Listen to this. James Kraft of Chicago has a patent for processed cheese."

"Processed cheese? What is that?"

"Pasteurized cheese that shan't spoil, so that it can be shipped. I need to discuss this with Hiram. This is an incredible advancement in shipping cheese to the troops. We need a contract with this Kraft fellow."

"Have you not enough investments to worry about?"

"You do remember our recent contract for stainless steel. Dear, one can never fail with a good investment."

"Yes, darling. I guess I must agree; my relationship with you was the best investment that I ever made. Now, I have the perfect father for my children," she said, patting her belly. She cringed a little.

"And you dare not forget it, Mrs. McDonnally."

They exchanged loving smiles. She continued knitting and he kept reading.

She looked up. "I would have preferred the investment in Pyrex cookware over stainless steel for gun barrels."

He glanced over the paper edge. "Yes, my dear, you are on record for that preference. We shan't go into that, again."

He dropped the paper to his lap. "Why cannot people get along?" he mumbled. "Here is a perfectly intelligent man—a genius in his own right, suffering at the hands of pure, senseless prejudice."

"Who would that be?"

"Garrett Morgan, the founder of the National Safety Device Company."

"I heard about him. He rescued thirty or more workers from shafts beneath that lake in the United States."

"Lake Erie."

"What happened to him?"

"Despite his life-saving invention, that twenty minute breathing device, which, I might add, rescue workers purchased gratefully, everywhere—his sales have plummeted."

"But why?"

"The public discovered that he is of the Negro race."

"That is utterly ridiculous—ignorant."

"'Tis. Now, many lives will be lost without the availability of his device."

Edward continued reading.

Then he muttered, "So, Mr. John D. Rockefeller, the first billionaire, enjoy it while you can—the McDonnallys are not far behind."

"Oh, *Edward*." She dropped her knitting. "OH, Edward! It is time!"

After a great deal of frantic chaos, the butler, Jules, sent word to Dr. Lambert and McDonnally Manor. Naomi was insistent that Hannah report for duty, since Naomi's mother, Beatrice was still in Ireland.

The scene was typical; the "out of control, to a great degree" exhausted father-to-be was pacing the halls. Sleepless, Hiram and Rahzvon joined him at Brachney Hall for support and comfort. Livia and Sophia had the triplets and Kade bedded down on the third floor. Unfortunately, Allison had gone to Langford with Trina and was none the wiser to the situation at home.

"Take it easy, ol' man. Women have been bearing children for thousands of years," Hiram attempted to reassure Edward.

"Not Naomi and she is *old*," Edward countered.

Rahzvon dropped to the divan, mumbling, "Glad she is not here to witness that comment."

Edward grabbed Hiram's lapel. "It has been too long! Do you think that she is having twins?"

"Nay, nay. I highly doubt it."

Rahzvon yawned. "I don't know. Sophia took a long time and she had three."

"Triplets," Edward screeched. "I am not ready for three—we have only one little cot!"

Hiram gripped Edward's forearms. "Calm down! No one said anything about triplets!"

Rahzvon leaned over the divan pillow. "I did." He closed his eyes.

"Ignore him, Edward. Come sit down, here in the rocking chair. Now, let us discuss something else. Anything newsworthy?"

Edward, drumming his fingers on the rocker arm, leaned back, then forward. He focused on Hiram. "What do you think of Einstein's new theory of general relativity?"

Hiram tilted his head. *I asked for that.* He cleared his throat. "I do not...Do you realize that

Ford has produced its millionth motor car?"

Wrinkles formed between Edward's brows. "Motorcar...I should have bought one—Naomi should not have had to ride in a carriage, bumping and bopping," he lamented.

"Edward, they have stop signs in Detroit, now!"

"Make it stop!" Naomi's shriek resounded throughout the mansion.

Edward flew from the chair and started for the staircase before Hiram deterred him. He noted the beads of perspiration forming on Edward's face.

"Steady man. The pain is natural."

Eloise, despite her many years, scurried by and up the steps, toting pails of hot water and linens. Edward watched and cringed. Pinching the bridge of his nose, he closed his eyes and mumbled, "I do not think that I can do this."

Hiram patted his back. "You do not have to—Naomi will. Man, you are as white as a specter. Rahzvon! Rahzvon, wake up!"

"Are they here?" he asked groggily.

"Nay. Make yourself useful. Get Edward a drink—some tea or something."

Rahzvon stretched and headed lazily toward the kitchen. Hiram guided the expectant father to the divan and sat next to him.

"Have you chosen any names?" Hiram said cheerily.

"Names?"

"For the bairn."

"Uh...aye."

"Well, what are they?"

"'Tis silly."

"Silly?"

"If it's a boy, she wants to name him Lucas."

"Ah, your pseudo identity. And for a lassie?

Rahzvon appeared in the doorway. "Hey, Papa, Eloise says that the doctor wants to see you upstairs."

"He—she is here?" Edward shouted.

"I do not think so."

"Oh." Edward turned slowly toward the staircase. Hiram offered a steadying arm to raise him from the seat.

"Come along, we will take it slowly," Hiram said, walking him to the first step.

"Help me, Hiram."

Hiram nodded and the two ascended toward the landing where the doctor waited and explained.

"Naomi asked to see you."

"Is the baby here?" Edward asked weakly.

"Not yet—but it shan't be too much longer. Only for a few minutes, now."

Hiram gave Edward a gentle nudge toward the master bedchamber. Edward stood facing the bed where his exhausted wife reached out to him.

"How are you love?" he asked, taking her hand and sitting down next to her.

"Dear, I want to tell you that I love you and that—"

"I love you too, my dear."

"Darling, if anything goes wrong—"

"Nothing shall go wrong. I promise you."

"But if it does, you do not have to raise our child alone."

"Naomi, stop. You and the bairn will be fine.

"Edward, it is alright if you remarry, but promise me that she shall be a good mother for our baby."

"Enough of this, I shan't discuss life without you. Now, you rest, I—"

The doctor stepped in. "Edward, ye need to be goin' back downstairs, now."

Edward swallowed hard. "Love, be brave and keep the faith. I shall see you *both* very soon." He leaned over and kissed her.

The door closed behind him as he entered the hall. Naomi's piercing scream dropped him to his knees and he sobbed uncontrollably, latched onto Hiram's sleeve. "Hiram, she thinks that she is going to leave me. I cannot live without her. She knows things," he cried.

Hiram knelt down beside him.

"Pray with me, Edward. Our, Father, who art in Heaven, hallowed be thy name. Thy kingdom come, thy will be done on earth—"

A tiny cry emulated from the other side of the door. Edward froze. His child had arrived safely, but what about Naomi? They slowly rose to their feet. The door opened and Hannah stepped out.

"Edward, Naomi and your bairn are well."

Edward turned to Hiram's embrace and broke down, again. The stoic twin who seldom revealed her emotions wiped her eyes with her handkerchief.

"The doctor will come for you when you can see them," she explained and disappeared behind the door.

Edward had pulled himself together and Hiram shook his hand.

"Congratulations, ol' man! You have two on me, now," he laughed." "You beat me to the alter, and now this."

"Thank you, Hiram, for being here, for me," he sniffled.

"I would not have been anywhere else."

Rahzvon scrambled up the stairs, when Dr. Lambert opened the door and stepped out with Hannah.

"Come in, Edward. Your wife has company," he said, smiling.

Edward entered; the doctor and Hannah remained in the hall, closing the door behind them.

Chapter XIV

"Out of the Mouths of Babes"

"If you must play,
Decide upon three things at the start:
the rules of the game,
the stakes, and the quitting time."

—Chinese proverb

"A laddie or a lassie, doctor?" Hiram asked eagerly.

"One, two, or three?" Rahzvon chimed in.

"That would be for the parents to announce," Dr. Lambert said, wiping his brow. "Now, please excuse me, I am in need o' some tea."

"Tell me, Hannah," Hiram insisted.

"You heard the doctor, Hiram. Dr. Lambert, I am going with you."

He offered his arm and the two walked down the stairs.

"Hannah! You are my twin—I have as much right to know as you!" His pleas were ignored.

"Dare to make a little wager," Rahzvon snickered.

"Twins? I would bet eight pounds that they are. Everyone is behaving a wee bit mysteriously, in my opinion."

"You are on."

Hiram, with knitted brows, studied Rahzvon's satisfied grin.

Rahzvon felt confident that there was no chance of twins in his comparative analysis of Naomi and Sophia. Sophia was at least three times the size of Naomi in her pregnancy. He highly doubted that Naomi had been carrying even two. They sealed the deal with a handshake and set off to notify Sophia and Livia of the new arrival.

Naomi smiled sweetly at her loving husband and pulled back the blanket.

"Smitty, meet your father."

"It is—I mean she is a girl?" he asked, beaming.

"Yes, darling and she is perfect, from her

silken hair to her tiny toes."

"Of course, she is. It must have been difficult for you; she is quite a handful...in a good way. She is much bigger than the triplets were."

"Yes, she is a healthy eight pounds even."

"You are going to need to knit a pair of pink stockings for her."

Naomi smiled and wiped away the single tear trickling down his cheek.

He leaned over and kissed her, then the hand of his tiny daughter. "What a little beauty. Love, can I show Hiram and Rahzvon? They were grand chaps, helping me through all of this."

"Certainly, but take care to support her head," she warned, handing him the bundle.

Hiram and Rahzvon were at the end of the hall discussing the blessed event with Sophia and Livia, when the proud father appeared in the hall. The four rushed to greet him with wide-eyed wonder. Edward pulled back the corner of the blanket.

"Meet the newest McDonnally—Smitty."

"A son! Congrats!" Rahzvon slapped him on the back.

"Nay—" Edward began.

"Yes, he is adorable," Livia grinned, stroking the tiny fingers.

"Nay—" Edward tried again.

"He is incredibly handsome and a good size," Sophia remarked.

"Nay...but yes, eight pounds even."

"Only one?" Hiram asked disapprovingly.

"Just one, but—"

"Ah, I win!" Rahzvon exclaimed.

Hiram's smile faded. "Nay, I said eight

pounds. And he weighs exactly eight pounds! Correct, Papa?"

"Yes, but—"

"You owe me eight pounds, Sierzik!"

"That was not the bet!" Rahzvon shouted.

"Sh! You were betting on that precious, little, innocent boy?" Sophia scorned.

"He said there were two! Nothing about weight!" Rahzvon argued.

"Shame on you, both!" Livia cut in.

"Pay up, Sierzik! You shook on it!" Hiram commanded.

"I will not!"

Edward slipped from the combat zone with his "son" and returned to his wife.

"What did they think?" Naomi asked excitedly.

"They think that she is a boy," he said solemnly.

Two weeks later, the morning started out like any other for the Sierzik household. Sophia had sent Rahzvon off on his route and the mother of three began preparing breakfast for them while they played in the baby-safe, couchless, parlor. The rocking chair was transported upstairs on the day before, when Sophia found Ruthia standing in it, rocking madly. The danger was not limited to Ruthia's welfare, but to her brother Von's who was sitting by the rocker attempting to retrieve a toy which was stuck underneath it. Sophia, nearly had heart failure at the sight. She tied the waists of the three adventurers to the table legs with a half-dozen diapers and lugged the chair upstairs. She made no mention of the account to her husband for fear he would think that she was an irresponsible parent. The rocking chair was reported as "needed" in the nursery upstairs.

She hummed while she stirred the porridge with the wooden spurtle, stirring stick, wondering how things were going at Brachney Hall with the newest family member. Then it happened—the unexpected: Zanya's shrill scream and her instant appearance in the kitchen doorway.

"Von is outside!"

Sophia dropped the stirrer and ran to the front door. She raced outside where she saw her tiny son standing by the road with arms outstretched to a man in a wagon.

"Von, NO!" she screeched.

Von turned and toddled toward her. The stranger slapped the reins and drove off like a bat out of Hades. Sophia dropped down to her baby and held him tightly to her chest. She was crying so hard that she could not stop. Von, who had never witnessed his mother in such an emotional state, began crying too.

"Vonnie, you never go outside without Mama or Daddy. That man could have taken you away forever," she sobbed. "I cannot imagine life without you."

Zanya stood on the step watching the drama.

A small hand touched Sophia's neck from behind.

"Mama, Von is safe."

Sophia stopped. She turned slowly to her daughter. Her jaw dropped.

"He was right...you *can* talk." Sophia stared at Zanya in awe. "Can you say something to Mama?"

"What should I say?" she said with a confused expression.

Her little sweet voice set Sophia's heart racing. "Zanya, my baby, thank you for saving your brother. This is all my fault. I knew that he was taller than you and your sister and that he could reach—" She stopped short. *Ruthia*—she was alone in the house with the hot porridge. She snatched a child under each arm and toted them into the house, yelling. "Stay away from the stove, Ruthia!"

Fortunately, Ruthia, oblivious to the breakfast cooking in the kitchen, entertained herself by teething on the handle of an umbrella pulled from the stand in the hall.

Hiram sat in the study at his desk, focused on his new bride. She was sitting on the floor, building a castle of wooden blocks with Thomas Kade.

"Livy?"

She looked up.

"I am so very sorry that we did not go on a holiday after the wedding."

"A honeymoon? As you said, dear, we will ...later."

"It is always 'later' with us, Livy."

She only smiled.

"I can only imagine how things went last night for Naomi and Edward without Hannah's help."

"I am certain that they were all just fine."

"Livy, it is such an age spread between Allison and wee Smitty. I think Kade should have a brother or sister... closer to his age."

She smiled again, but did not comment.

That very afternoon, Sophia, proud mother,

drove her three bairns to Lochmoor Glen while Rahzvon was on his postal route. This was breaking news that could not wait. She entered the McDonnally estate drive at top speed to share her discovery with her mother, Hiram, Livy and everyone else in the village.

One minute Sophia was in the carriage with the triplets; the next, she was in the entrance hall with Zanya in tow. Sophia was calling in desperation, "Mama! Uncle Hiram, Livia! Eloise, Miles!"

The housekeeper, Eloise was the first to appear.

"What is it Sophia?" she asked in near panic.

"Where is everyone? I need to speak with them, immediately!"

"The Master and Mrs. McDonnally are in the study with young Kade."

"Where is my mother?"

"In the garden, writing a letter to Mr. Candole."

Sophia flew past her and flung open the backdoor.

"Mother, come quickly!"

Hannah dropped her pen and ran toward the house. "What has happened? Is the baby alright?" she called to her daughter, running toward the study.

"Yes!" Sophia stopped midway to pick up Zanya whose tiny steps could not keep up.

Eloise called to her, too. "Where are the other two?"

Sophia paused at the pocket doors. "Great Scott, they are still in the carriage! Please bring them in!" She then knocked and shoved the study doors open. Hannah raced in behind her. Sophia stood puffing from the hall jaunt and ran over to Livia.

"I want to enroll Zanya in the first grade."

Livia smiled. "Why certainly, when the triplets are six years of age, there will definitely be a place for them."

"No, no, no. I want to enroll her, now!"

"But she is not even two, as yet."

Hiram began laughing; Livia held back her smiles and Hannah shook her head.

Eloise stood in the doorway with a small Sierzik hand clinging to each of hers. "Attending school at one year?" Eloise questioned.

"You laugh, but this is serious! My sweet Zanya is a genius. She saved her brother's life!" She turned to Von. He offered a broad clueless smile.

Hiram, who had shown some self-restraint to hear her out, burst into laughter, again.

Hannah put a comforting hand on her daughter's shoulder. "*Sophia.*"

The condescending tone enraged her. She pulled away; her black eyes blazed with fury.

"Now, all of you listen to me. This child can speak flutently!"

"*Fluently,*" her mother gently corrected her.

"She can speak in full sentences—in paragraphs!"

The room got quiet.

"My husband will verify it. I did not believe him until this morning. She told me that Von was outside. He would have been kidnapped, had she not warned me."

Now, the audience would have liked to believe

her, but it was a matter of her crying wolf. After Sophia's elaborate account of the twister, they had mixed feelings about her credibility and story-telling ability.

"Well, let's hear her," Hiram challenged her.

Sophia stood frozen, knowing that Zanya may not speak on command. She refused for her father, that first day and she had not spoken a single word on the trip from home.

"She, she only speaks when she wants to. She is not a dog that barks on command!" Sophia scoffed.

"Put her down, Sophia," Hiram said, motioning with his hand.

She lowered her to the floor.

"Zanya, come here to Great Uncle Hiram," he gently coaxed.

She stood motionless with a firm grip on the hem of her mother's skirt. She then shrugged and looked away.

Hiram leaned back in his chair and raised a dubious brow.

"Ask her a question, Mother," Sophia insisted.

"Zanya, what are the names of your sister and brother?"

Zanya glanced at her grandmother and giggled.

"Livia, you are good with children. Ask her something," Sophia pleaded.

"Uh...what is your name?"

Zanya ignored her inquiry and was now focused on Kade and the castle.

"Very well, do not believe me, but I still want her enrolled in the first grade, immediately! She needs to learn to read and write!"

Livia looked at Sophia sympathetically.

"I understand that you are trying to do the best thing for your children, but she is much too young to—"

"Never mind! I shall teach her myself! Come along, Zanya."

Sophia marched to the door and leaned down to pick up her silent child.

Zanya turned to the disbelievers, "Goodbye. I shall see you all later."

Sophia raised her head slowly, grinning like a Cheshire cat. She hugged her genius daughter, stuck out her tongue at the flabbergasted audience, and disappeared into the hall.

Only time would tell what would become of the quick witted, little Zanya and her siblings—Ruthia and Vonmanstrong.

During the week following November 11, 1918, the Lochmoor Glen residents boarded an emotional roller coaster. The news of the signing of the Treaty of Versailles, ending the Great War, brought a plethora of mixed feelings. The relief was overwhelming. This new time of peace would present an abundance of possibilities and opportunities for those of the quaint village.

The day that Tavy and Guillaume arrived from the Shueburyness War Dog School was one of great celebration. Both sets of adoptive parents, the Dugans and the Zigmanns burst into tears at the sight of their returning sons. Although the young men were not engaged in actual warfare, they had been gone for two years.

Tavy embraced Harriet and Joseph with one

eye on the little boy who he had left behind. Rufus was a head taller and had lost his juvenile facial characteristics.

"Carrot Top, I see that ye hae done a good job trainin' yer best friend," Tavy said, slowly approaching him.

Rufus nodded, holding the lead rope to the quiet, immobile donkey.

Tavy and Rufus stood awkwardly facing each other with what seemed to be the years of unspoken words still between them. Tavy extended his hand to him. Rufus's eyes welled up. He dropped the lead, ran to Tavy and cried as if he were five years old again.

"We hae a lot o' time to make up for—a lot o' fishin'," Tavy said, wiping his escaping tears with one hand and hugging Rufus with the other.

Tavy looked up to meet the longing eyes of the faithful Trina Dunmore. Beyond her, Mercy was laughing with the Zigmanns and the McDonnally clan, surrounding Guillaume. Then Mercy turned toward Tavy. Suddenly, in a moment of clarity, they realized that all the love they shared remained intact.

Trina approached him. "Hello, sailor."

"Trina." He gave her a warm embrace, but nothing more. She knew at that melancholy moment that there was no future with him and Rufus. Two long years of corresponding was not enough to land Henry McTavish.

Tavy was distracted by Hannah's aloofness from the welcoming clan. Trina slipped away, unnoticed, to join the McDonnallys welcoming Guillaume.

Tavy turned to Harriet. "Ma, any word from

Oscar?"

"Nay, son," she said sadly.

His remorse was cut short by a gentle tap on the shoulder. He turned to the delighted countenance of Mrs. Eck Huntley.

"Welcome home, lad."

He shook her hand. "Mrs. Huntley, how hae ye been?"

"Henry, I am doin' wonderfully, thanks to yer lad, here."

"Rufus?"

"Aye, he has been a great help. I'm goin' to miss his daily visits. He's been good company, runnin' errands and workin' round me cottage, since ye left. He filled in for some of Master McDonnally's chores when he had taken ill."

"Aye?" He turned to Rufus, now stroking Pete's mane. Tavy felt an immense pride in being the boy's father.

"Take some time for ye and the lad!" she suggested as she waved goodbye.

Three little McDonnally-looking faces appeared by Pete's side.

"May we pet him, Rufus? May we?" they pleaded.

Tavy was awestruck, again. The Sierzik triplets were no longer infants. Before he had a chance to ask them about their parents, they arrived.

"Gypsy, Miss Muffet! Ah! Ye two hae been busy."

Sophia blushed with one hand on her enlarged waistline.

"Need another son to even it up, Gypsy?" Tavy teased, embracing Rahzvon. "Ye may get three more lassies!" he laughed.

"Do not even mention it!" Rahzvon warned, and then smiled.

Tavy glanced at Allison and Adam sitting on a bench.

"Sophia, I see that you and Allison, finally have something or should I say a wee someone, in common."

"Yes, we do. We are the best of friends, now. The four of us spend a lot of time together. Sorry you missed Allison and Adam's wedding. I helped with it and I was matron of honor. Rahzie was best man. It was small and quaint, but positively romantic—not as romantic as mine and Rahzie's, but lovely."

Tavy flashed back on the day prior to that happy event when he thought Sophia and Rahzvon had broken it off and he had planned to propose to her.

"Uh,,.this Monroe chap is a good man?" Tavy asked.

"The best," Rahzvon assured him. "He will be a great father, as well."

"Sophia, I am sorry about Oscar."

"We all are, but we shan't give up hope...Jake will be returning in a few months. You shall have to attend their wedding. Agnes is beside herself with excitement. Rahzie where are the children?"

"Over there." He pointed across the green. "They are following Rufus and Pete."

"We need to fetch our brood. Welcome home, again." Sophia stood on tiptoe and kissed his cheek.

"Take care! I think six bairns is enough!" Edward interrupted carrying his pride and joy. "Welcome home, Tavy."

"Thank ye, Edward." He shook his free hand.

"So this is the much bigger Smitty."

"Yes, she's growing like a weed. The McDonnally genes."

"So are ye prepared to be a new pa and grandpa at the same time?"

"He'll manage," Naomi cut in. "Welcome home, Henry."

"Yer as beautiful as ever, Naomi. So is this little lassie. The war has certainly increased the bairn population," he remarked, seeing Bruce carrying an infant. "Tell me that it is a son."

Edward spoke up, "It is. But being the only male in the family, is not so bad. I feel privileged."

"Oh, *Edward*," Naomi shoved him playfully.

Tavy noted Hiram standing next to Livia. "I see Hiram and Livia havena added a playmate for Kade." Naomi's smile vanished.

She said in a hushed tone, "Henry, they lost their first, but are trying again. Please do not say anything. Only the family knows. I just did not want you to say anything to them, as they took it very hard. Hiram was not himself for some time."

Tavy remembered Mrs. Huntley's comment about Rufus filling in for Hiram.

"I'm sorry to hear it. Hiram's a tough man, but 'tis a difficult blow. I shan't say anything. How are yer mother and Daniel?"

"They have returned to Ireland to be with family—a reunion of sorts. The Stricklands have gone with them. Abigail is meeting them there."

"Did I miss that wedding, too?"

"No, Mother and Daniel have temporarily postponed it. Well, Henry, we need to get this little one home for a nap."

"Good to see ye."

"You, too. You will have to bring Rufus and Trina to supper some evening."

Tavy only smiled. He felt eyes upon him. He slowly turned to see Mercy standing before him.

"Hello, Henry."

He studied her face and then took her hand in his.

In the distance, Rufus watched with his fingers crossed and a hopeful smile while his Pa and Mercy walked to the opposite side of the village green.

"Come on, Rufus! Bring Pete o'er here!" Jeanie Wheaton called, waving by the park bench on which Zanya, Von, and Ruthia were standing, fighting for position for the first donkey ride.

"Hurry Rufus! It is gettin' ugly!" Jeanie shouted.

Nevertheless, Rufus, leading Pete, paused midway when he saw Kade running toward him.

"May I please, have a ride, Rufus?"

"Aye, mount up." The three then trotted off to the awaiting, anxious triplets.

"Why did *he* get to go first?" Ruthia demanded, when they arrived. "I was supposed to be first!"

"Oh, hush, Ruthia," Zanya cut in.

Von rolled his eyes and shook his head.

"Because he was in the right place at the right time," Rufus explained and then glanced back at his Pa and Mercy, locked in what seemed a never-ending kiss. "Aye, the right place at the right time." He grinned ear-to-ear.

"May I print a kiss on your lips?" I asked;
She nodded her sweet permission:
So we went to press, and I rather guess
We printed a large edition."

—Anonymous

To the readers of my series:

I want to thank you for your interest in my novels and I hope that I have met your expectations for your visits to Lochmoor Glen. This is the final novel in the Lochmoor Glen series. I normally have several titles for each new novel, before making the final choice. With this novel, I had none. Then it came to me, Life Without You. It seemed to be the perfect fit. What I didn't know was that, ten days later, I would unexpectedly lose my beloved horse of seventeen years.

The void and shock was, as my family said, "like losing one of my children." My life will never be the same. Kazimir Jacque Khali, beautiful bay, Percheron/Arab cross was a very intelligent, loving, sensitive companion,. He was quick to learn ground games that I created and enjoyed playing them. He was always in tune to my feelings and moods. He helped me through difficult life changes. He was a gentle leader in every herd that he met in his travels to different boarding facilities. Finally, thanks to David, for one short year, our dream came true—he came home to live with us.

The empty place in my heart is slowly filling with the wonderful memories that we shared. Kaz, like his buddy, Baron, has gone to live forever in Lochmoor Glen as "Hunter." I dedicate this series to him, my sweet, gentle giant.

I hope you will enjoy my next series, which may answer any questions about the future of the characters, who you have come to know and enjoy. God willing, the first novel in the Beyond Lochmoor Glen series will be available in 2016.

Bless you, Arianna Snow

In 1903, Andrew Jackson Jr. invented protective hen goggles.

Actual meanings of the names and Scottish traits are mentioned at the tea.

Actual accounts of trench life and tetanus epidemic are recorded by "Jake."

Planters Peanut Co. founded in 1906. Fourteen-year old Antonio Gentile designed Mr. Peanut for five dollars.

There is a superstition that it is bad luck to see a pig en route to the church, which is resolved by returning to the origin and beginning the journey again.

The pinning of the bride with the clan badge, the sword and horseshoe presentations and sharing of the bride's cog(drink made from hot ale, whiskey, beaten eggs, and sugar— served in half barrel with handles) are Scottish wedding customs.

The following were popular magazines: *Lady's Realm* magazine 1896-1915 *Photoplay (film magazine)* 1911-1963 *The Camp Magazine* Diary of British prisoners at Groningen

Thirty-nine Steps is a novel by John Buchan-Scot. Lawrence's *The Rainbow* is a novel about the dynasty of farmers and craftsmen in England.

The Thermos (heat in Greek), "vacuum flask" was invented by James Dewar in 1907.

Jacob David sold the idea to make trousers from Levi Strauss cloth, jeans ("gene" from Genoa France) in 1873.

8.7 knots = approx. 10 mph

Rufus routinely recites actual British nursery rhymes.

The Irish crown Jewels were stolen from Dublin Castle in 1907. The protecting guards were executed and the jewels were never found.

The details of the town of Clovelly in southern England, and the donkey's behavior are true. The legend of the donkey "Cross" is one marking him as a loyal and loving creature.

The Panama hat, sailor blouses, military style suits for women, plain broad brimmed hats without former plumage for women, layered angular hemmed skirts, elaborate embroidery on dresses, and toy horses on wheeled platforms were popular at this time.

The references to the two extraordinary horses, Sampson and Old Billy of England are actual accounts.

The facts of the life of Alexander MacKenzie, storekeeper/photographer are given in Chapter XI.

Pete's "outfitting" is a true account of the author's Christmas "Miniature donkey" gift from her better half.

Holyrood Park was created in 1541 in central Edinburgh, Scotland.

Wemyss means "cave."

Finnan toasties and powsawdie is smoked haddock and sheep's head broth. Cabbie-claw is wind-dried cod with horseradish and egg sauce.

Pollyanna Grows Up is a novel written by Eleanor H. Porter in 1915.

Punch is a 1840-2002 British magazine of humor and satire.

During the Great War, women generally took over the postal routes.

United States purchased the Virgin Islands.

Scottish grace was recited at Mrs. Monroe's table.

Salmon fishing on the River Dee and trout fishing in the West Highlands was common.

Lime washing is a practice to protect and renew the exterior of cottages.

Women suffragists were in fact arrested at the White House and the account of Emily Dawson, suffragist is true.

The First battle of Somme and Quay Easter Rising are real accounts.

Shueburyness was a war dog training school.

Bat Masterson was appointed U.S. Marshall of the Arizona Territory by President Roosevelt.

The Bachelor Bill Military Service Act required those unmarried men ages 18 to 41 to report for service,

In 1916 Kraft obtained patent for processed cheese.

In 1912 Stainless steel "Staybrite" was used for gun barrels.

Pyrex, by Corning, was introduced in 1915.

News of J.D. Rockefeller being first billionaire was true.

The details of Garrett Morgan/inventor in 1916 are accurate.

A spurtle is a popular Scottish wooden, rod-shaped kitchen utensil made from maple, invented around the 15th century.

Poetry Excerpts from the Chapters

Acknowledgements

British English A to Zed. New York: Facts on File, Inc., 2001.

Chronicle of the 20th Century. New York: Chronicle Publications, 1987.

Grun, Bernard. The Timetables of History: A Horizontal Linkage of People and Events. New York: Simon and Schuster, 1982.

Illustrated Encyclopedia of Scotland. Anacortes: Oyster Press, 2004.

Kirkby, Mandy. Pick Your Brains About Scotland. London: Cargan Guides, 2005.

Lacayo, Richard & George Russell. Eyewitness 150 Years of Journalism. New York: Time Inc. Magazine Company, 1995.

Library of Curious and Unusual Facts. Alexandria,Virginia: Time-Life Books, 1990.

Livingstone, Sheila. Scottish Customs. New York: Barnes & Noble Books, 1996.

Summers, Gilbert. Exploring Rural Scotland. Lincolnwood: Passport Books, 1996.

The American Heritage History of World War I. New York. Simon and Shuster. 1964

This Fabulous Century Volume I and II. New York: Time-Life Books, 1969.

Webster's New Explorer Desk Encyclopedia. Springfield, MA: Federal Street Press, 2003.

Worthington-Williams, Michael. The Scottish Motor Industry. Great Britain: Shire Publications Ltd.,1989.

*I am a firm believer that education
should be an ongoing endeavor.
I stand by the unwritten law that education
should be entertaining for young and old, alike.
Thus, I incorporate
historic places, people, and events in my novels,
for your learning pleasure.*

*With loving thoughts,
Arianna Snow*

To order copies
of the
Lochmoor Glen Series

Visit the
Golden Horse Ltd.
website:
www.ariannaghnovels.com

Watch for the first in the
new series:

Beyond Lochmoor Glen